ISBN-13: 978-1-7337467-9-3

Though this book is set in England, it holds to the American English conventions.
This book contains explicit content and graphic language.
For mature audiences only.

THE CHARING CROSS BOYS

Book Three

I Put a Spell on You

M. KATHERINE CLARK

Other Works by M. Katherine Clark

The Greene and Shields Files

Love Among the Shamrocks Collection

Love Among the Shamrocks Collection the Next Generation

Love Among the Shamrocks Universe

The Charing Cross Boys

      Set Fire to the Rain

      Sweet Caroline

      I Put a Spell on You

      Hold Me Closer – *Coming Soon*

      You Don't Own Me – *Coming Soon*

The Wolf's Bane Saga

Dragon Fire

Sherlock Holmes Family

MacCulloch Castle Ghosts

For all my fans, thank you for your support of my boys! I am so excited to share not only Boyd and Vidar's story, but also Rhys and Kiter, Gabe and Sweet, Callum and Killian, and Dae-Hyun, Gareth, and Elton! I love being able to write something you all enjoy!

And to the ladies of Haven!! Thank you for your encouragement!

Prologue

The noises coming from Boyd's room were in human.

Vidar Jørgensen saw the play by play in his mind simply by the identifiable sounds Boyd and Sasha, their Russian contact, were making. The Russian wasn't quiet, praising Boyd's *tight little hole* and telling him what a *good boy* he was for *Daddy.*

Ugh!

Vidar pulled the pillow from behind his head and tried to muffle the sounds of Boyd orgasming... again. But it didn't help. Everything played like a movie in his mind's eye, and it made him... sad? Frustrated? Horny? Angry? He wasn't sure. Boyd had turned his head from the first moment he had seen him. There was something about that man that twisted him up inside. He wanted to protect him, claim him, pin him down, and make love to him all at once. He needed Boyd to look at him, talk to him, turn that flirtation to him, more than he needed his next breath. But Boyd clearly didn't feel the same about him.

Finally hearing Sasha finish should have given him a moment's reprieve but with the quiet came the picture of Boyd and Sasha, sweaty, nude, covered in cum, and panting. *Are they cuddling?* Would Sasha leave? Would they share intimacies? Would they simply bask in their mutual satiation?

With a frustrated grunt, Vidar ripped the pillow off his face, pealed the bed sheets off, and stood. He grabbed a pair of joggers and slid them on. Ignoring his erection, he tried to will it away as he headed to the door. He needed water... *or a bottle of Scotch,* he thought, to get the images out of his mind. Opening the door of his bedroom, he walked down the short corridor to the kitchen in the underground safe house in Târgu Mureş, Transylvania.

Stopping short when he saw his teammates and boss, standing around the island with bottles or cans of something to drink.

"Heya," his boss, Sommerset Kiter greeted him. Seeing his teammates, he instantly moved his hands to cover his erection. "You made it out of there. We wondered how long you could take the abuse."

"You all heard it?" Vidar asked.

"Hard not to," Rhys, Kiter's boyfriend, said. "Boyd isn't shy, and it sounds like Sasha isn't either."

"We all decided the kitchen was the safest place. The sounds are muffled here," Gabe said. Vidar considered Gabe a close friend, even after only a week as they found common ground. Like Vidar, Gabe had only just recently understood his sexuality as something other than straight.

Nigel, Gabe's boyfriend, walked over to him, a soft pitying smile lifting his perfect lips. He offered a water bottle. "Thanks,"

Vidar accepted.

"Are you all right?" Nigel asked, his slight Caribbean accent teasing and lilting the words. "Do you need something stronger?"

"I'd take a bottle of the good stuff if we weren't on a mission right now," Vidar muttered. Nigel squeezed his arm.

Before any of them could say anything more, the door opened, and heavy footsteps echoed down the corridor. Sasha turned the corner with a smirk on his stupid, ruggedly handsome face. He paused only a moment to take in the faces looking at him. His jeans were slung low on his hips, and it was clear he wore no pants as the top of his pubic hair was visible.

"Evening," he said as he headed to the refrigerator and pulled on the door.

Pretentious prick.

Sasha pulled the cap off some juice and chugged. The way his throat moved; Vidar remembered the sounds he heard when Boyd cried out earlier talking nonsense. Again, Vidar shook his head. He didn't want to think about it, nor did he want to explore why his joggers were still tight.

No one spoke as Sasha drank, beads of sweat trickling down his chest. He lowered the carton and looked at everyone. "What?" He questioned. The team shrugged collectively and turned away. "Is something matter?" His Russian accent was very strong.

Rhys and Gabe shook their heads and looked away. Nigel took a breath as if to speak, looking at Vidar, but Vidar stopped him. "Could you try and keep it down next round?" He asked. "My room is right next door and I'm trying to sleep."

A salacious grin lifted Sasha's lips. "Sorry about that. But you're welcome. It's not every day you get to listen to something so hot."

"Sash?" Boyd's voice preceded him. Vidar couldn't stop himself. He looked. "Oh, sorry."

Shite.

Boyd wore Sasha's white t-shirt and only the white t-shirt. It fell to his mid-thigh. His face was flushed, he glistened with euphoria and a bit of sweat. He had hickeys bitten and sucked into his beautifully pale skin. The reddest one at his neck but Vidar's eyes drifted lower and there were two reddening marks on his inner thighs. The water bottle in his hand crinkled loudly in the silence. Vidar looked away.

"Are you coming back?" He asked Sasha.

"I'll be right there, малыш," Sasha said. It was a beat later when Vidar heard Sasha continue. "Well, gentlemen, as nice as this has been, I have other things to do tonight. Good night." With that, Sasha tossed the now empty carton into the trash and headed down the corridor. He turned just before the corner and locked eyes with Vidar. "I told you earlier, you're not fit for this game. Boyd needs a man. One who knows what he's doing and one who can satisfy him. Not a boy who can't make up his mind. Take some pointers while listening and come back when you've grown into who you claim to be."

Vidar clenched his fists ready to wipe the ugly smile off Sasha's face. *Stop.* He ordered. *Not worth it,* rang in his mind. *He's telling the truth.* He didn't know how to satisfy Boyd. He'd never been with a man. He'd tried to talk to Boyd, but he always got tongue tied or his nerves would get the better of him and he'd chicken out. No matter what, Sasha was right, he wasn't man enough for Boyd.

Nigel gently touched his arm, and he jumped and turned.

"Take Gabe's and my room tonight, Vi. It's at the end of the corridor. We could barely hear it."

Gabe stepped up beside his boyfriend. "Yeah, honestly, it's no trouble."

"I need you sharp tomorrow, Vi," Kiter said. "You need to get some sleep. We're merely ten hours away from the bank heist."

As if mocking him, there was a squeal from Boyd's room followed by giggling. Vidar took a deep breath. "You don't mind?" He asked Nigel and Gabe.

"Not at all," Nigel promised, and Gabe shook his head.

"Thank you," he turned to head back to his room and get his things when Rhys' voice called out.

"Give it time. He sees you but there's... more to him than any of us know. He hides behind this façade but trust me when I say, underneath, there is a scared little boy needing to be gently coaxed out. He went through hell as a kid. Had to grow up fast."

So did I, Vidar thought.

"This is his way of rebelling," Rhys went on. "Be patient with him. You scare him."

"What? Why?" Vidar breathed out.

"Because you are his forever, and he doesn't know what to do about that."

Chapter One

The door was opening. Fourteen-year-old Boyd Falstaff knew what that meant, and he ducked down deeper into his threadbare mattress and lifted the single blanket up to his nose. Maybe he wouldn't be picked that time. Maybe someone else would. But that thought made him hate himself even more. He would never wish that on anyone, let alone any of the other boys in the room with him. Though he was small, he was stronger than any of them. He could handle it.

He heard a scream and clutched his grandfather's Victoria Cross medallion tighter in his hand. The youngest of them begged as the man dragged him toward the door. The boy was only nine years old. The man was a monster. They all were. But the boys were stuck there. Orphans. Wards of the state. He never thought he'd say it, but he missed the nuns. They at least never did that to them. But the church had been bought out by the state and they were long gone. Abandoned again.

"Please, no!" The boy begged but it was no use. The monsters never heard their pleas. They fed off them, watching as grown men took their pleasure for money. They took videos, pictures and sold them on something called the internet. Boyd didn't know what that was. They were kept away from all modern technologies like heat or central air, internet was just something else. "Please!"

Boyd gripped the medal so tightly, it cut the skin of his palm.

"Shut your mouth, boy or we'll have more fun with you," the voice of their nightmares said.

The boy whimpered. Boyd dared to look at the boys in the cot next to him. They were awake but cuddled close like he and Jack used to. Jack. Jack was gone. He was the eldest of all of them. He used to volunteer to save the young until they had beaten him so badly he bled everywhere and that was when Boyd had first experienced what the monsters did to them. But Jack was gone. No one had seen him for months. Without him, Boyd was the eldest.

"Please," the little boy whimpered again. He wasn't walking, the man was dragging him by the collar of his tattered pajama shirt. He was so young. "No!" The boy screamed and Boyd flinched when he heard the sound of the man's hand smacking the boy's face.

"Didn't I tell you to shut up?" the voice demanded.

The boy cried and Boyd knew what he had to do. What he had to do since Jack was gone. He needed to be their Jack.

Squeezing his eyes shut, he tucked his grandfather's medal under the mattress, and met the eyes of his friends who watched him. Silently, he asked them to watch his one possession. They agreed and he took a breath.

Give me strength, grandpa.

"Stop," Boyd called and with shaking fingers, he pulled the blanket off him and stood. The room went deathly still as if the other boys were afraid to breathe. "Let him go."

The monster was backlit by the light in the hallway holding the boy's arm. He couldn't see his face, but Boyd knew him. He knew every inch of him. The Warden, Jacob McMasters. "What are you doing?" The monster demanded. "Get back to bed."

"No," Boyd said. "Let him go... take... take me instead."

The very air seemed to be sucked out of the room and everything went deathly quiet.

Boyd woke in a cold sweat. A scream on the tip of his tongue as he took in the vaguely familiar surroundings. He wasn't home. He was in the MI6 bunker in the basement of HQ. He wasn't a little boy. He was a grown man. Taking a deep breath, he swallowed the bile that threatened to eject from his mouth. The dreams were as vivid as ever since he found out about Sasha's part in nearly killing one of his teammates. He felt used by the man. Disgusted. Abused. Just like when he was a boy. Hating the memories, he tried to dispel them like the shrink he had seen in his late teens had taught him. But her methods only worked when he was on the cusp of a panic attack, not when he was too far gone. The memories. The dreams. He needed to get away.

Pulling off the sheet, he grabbed his sweat soaked t-shirt

and tossed it in the bin. Grabbing a fresh one, he pulled it over his head and grabbed his yoga pants, tugging them on over his underpants. He opened the door as quietly as he could and left the room. The entire team and their families were living down there in safety until Sasha could be caught and he had no desire to wake his teammates, let alone their families. Padding down the hall, he quietly headed to the gym but stopped short of the door when he heard someone hitting the punching bag. The soft grunts of the man as he threw his body into the punch and the subtle *thunk* of his fists hitting the faux leather exterior and the tinkling of the thick chain that held the bag to the ceiling. He wasn't in the mood to talk or to be observed but he also didn't want to be alone. Maybe whoever it was felt the same.

The door squeaked as he pushed it open and the *thunks* stopped. Boyd entered the room and turned toward the punching bag. Callum O'Grady, their team leader, looked back at him. He breathed a sigh of relief and opened the door fully. If anyone would understand him at that moment, it would be Cal.

"Demons keeping you awake too?" Boyd asked. He had found a kindred soul in the team lead as they both knew what the other had been through.

"Something like that," Callum answered, his eyes showing the haunted look he sometimes had.

"Need someone to hold the bag? Or do you want to be left alone?"

Callum paused. "I have a better idea." Turning to the small ledge holding a bottle of water, his mobile, and some hand tape, "Wanna learn?" He asked tossing Boyd the roll of athletic tape.

"Sure, if you'll bear with me."

Callum nodded and Boyd walked over. Taking the end of

the tape, Callum offered to protect his knuckles and then found boxing gloves. Helping Boyd by tugging them on for him, Callum checked to make sure they were secure enough.

"Don't want to ruin your pretty hands, thief," Callum teased.

"Definitely not. Soft as kitten paws."

"And just as deadly."

"Don't know about that," Boyd chuckled. It was easy with Callum. They understood each other. There was no attraction, at least on his part, but Callum had given him no indication he liked him more than a friend. Boyd could be himself with Callum. They didn't need to act around each other. If one went quiet, the other understood the need to fight one's own demons.

Callum saddled up behind him and tapped his foot until he got in the right position. He then lifted Boyd's arms and helped him square up to the bag.

"Your dominant hand is your right, correct?"

"Yes," Boyd answered.

"Right, that's opposite for me but I'll try," he teased. "So you jab with your left. That's quick rapid hard hits to stun your opponent but you follow through with your right to really knock them down. So your left hand is One and your right is Two. So, if I wanted you to jab I'd call out One. Then a combo move of One-Two would be a jab and a punch with your right."

"Got it."

"You're small but strong, so you'll want to wait until they get close. Daze them with a jab to the nose or throat, soft tissue, then follow with a right across the jaw or toward the temple. For now, you'll want to focus on the bag. See where it's worn?" Boyd nodded. "That's going to be softer for you."

"It's pretty worn, how often do you do this?"

Callum let out a breath that tickled Boyd's ear. "Recently? Very. Now, square up," he walked behind the bag and held it. "Jab. One." Boyd did and struck the bag quickly with his left hand. "Good. But keep your right protecting your jaw. It can also be used to block." He reached across and moved Boyd's hand up to his jaw. "Good. One-Two." Callum called and Boyd hit the bag with the combo. "Stay loose. That's why a lot of people bounce while they do it. One-Two."

They continued that way for a few more minutes. Callum added a couple kicks to Boyd's combos. He had just gotten it correct, and Callum praised him, when the door to the gym opened and Vidar Jørgensen entered, their newest teammate and Boyd's... difficult obsession. He didn't *want* to like him. Vidar was so completely... his type. He'd deny it if he could but there was no reason. Every time the Norwegian walked by or was within eyesight, Boyd inevitably watched him. He drew him in like no one else. He fought his attraction to the handsome blonde, but he didn't understand why. He wasn't bad or evil like Sasha. There was just something about him that unnerved Boyd. He could be sweet one minute and harsh the next, but his eyes were always kind. Boyd wasn't used to kindness.

"Oh, sorry," Vidar said when he looked up and saw them.

"No, no, come on in," Callum replied waving him into the room. "I was just showing Boyd how to throw a few punches. What do you think of his form?"

Boyd watched Vidar walk over, his big body moving like a cat. He had natural grace and rhythm. He would have made one hell of a dancer if he had chosen. Instead, he was former Special Forces, Army, Special Reconnaissance Regiment. He was a killing machine and he looked hot doing it. *No, bad Boyd. Bad.* He shook his head.

"Boyd, square up," Callum called and instantly he did. He didn't know why but he wanted to impress Vidar. "And One... One-Two. Kick. One-Two. One. One. One. One-Two." Boyd followed the orders and had fun. Then, Callum turned to Vidar. "What do you think?"

Vidar stared, his eye critical. "Your kick is off center. You kick like that, and someone can catch your foot and the right person could break your ankle." He walked behind him and moved his arm. "Your jab needs to be turned out a bit more. And your right should extend from your shoulder not the elbow."

"He just started," Callum justified.

"Clearly," Vidar answered. "You're tiny, so you'll want to stand more like this." He moved him. "And your legs are shorter, so you'll need to make sure you only kick at shins and crotch."

"Ookay," Boyd sang. "I've had enough." He pulled off his boxing gloves. "Thank you, Callum for the lesson. I appreciate it." He handed the gloves back to him and turned a scathing look to Vidar. "And as for you, Ikea, you really could learn some niceties."

"Ikea?" Vidar questioned. "Seriously?"

Boyd shrugged. "Would make a great code name for you. Swedish, confusing as hell, yummy treats, made up of bits and pieces that make no sense. Yeah, I like IKEA better than Thor. Suits you better. I'm going to take a shower and grab a coffee." He walked toward the door.

After a beat, he heard Callum. "He just started, Vidar."

"Forget it, Cal," Boyd tossed over his shoulder. "Some people don't get it. Your father may have used degradation to teach you, Vidar, but not everyone likes it. I *was* having fun."

"Self-defense isn't something you get a second chance at," Vidar replied. "You must get it right the first time."

"Then, I guess it's a good thing Callum taught me to shoot because it's clear I'll never be good enough for you."

"That has nothing to do with—"

Boyd didn't let him finish. He walked out and let the door shut behind him, effectively ending the conversation. He let out a frustrated grunt and headed to the dressing room.

"Seriously?" Callum questioned as soon as the door shut behind Boyd. Vidar looked over at the Irishman.

"What?"

"I set you up with a perfect way to compliment him and get on his good side, and all you do is critique him and make him feel inferior."

"Self-defense is not something to compliment if you do it poorly. He hits a man like Sasha the way he was hitting that bag and he's dead before he hits the floor."

"You could have complimented his effort even if the execution wasn't up to par."

"What good is the effort if the execution isn't one hundred percent? Do it right or don't do it. It's as simple as that."

"Is that how your dad taught you?"

"Leave my father out of this."

"Why?" Callum crossed his arms over his chest. He was of medium build, but he and Vidar had sparred. Callum was strong. "He's the reason you don't embrace your bisexuality. He's the reason you started to defend yourself in the first place." *Damn him and his research.* Callum had recruited everyone on the team, at their boss's insistence. Callum knew too much. Or rather Vidar had revealed too much during their initial meeting. "Tell me," he went on. "Your dad was known for anger issues and playing dirty on the Pitch, then miraculously, he stopped picking fights during a game. Did he take it out on you?"

"You go too far, O'Grady. My father's and my relationship has nothing to do with this. Boyd needs to learn how to defend himself. I may not be around all the time."

"Oh, so that's it? You want him to learn how to protect himself because you are afraid of Sasha. You're afraid he'll come back for him."

"I'm not afraid. But it would be stupid not to be prepared. Sasha already nearly took out Nigel. I... I can't let him hurt Boyd too." Vidar huffed a sigh.

"Listen," Callum began after a moment of silence. "I know you think you'll always be tongue-tied around him. I know you think he deserves better than you. I know you worry about your father's reaction to finding out you're... not straight, but you can't take it out on Boyd. You do and you're no better than your father taking his anger out on you. Tell me, do you want to treat Boyd how your father treated you? Or do you want to understand the attraction you have to him and possibly let it go somewhere? Because a man like Boyd doesn't take kindly to being talked down to."

"I wasn't talking down to him."

"You may not think so, because of your experiences, but you were. You treated him like a child. And I know you see him as a grown man and not a child. So treat him as an equal. He may not be able to rip tree stumps in half with his bare hands, but he can do a lot of other things better than you. How would you feel if he

14

tore you down if you couldn't type the right hacker's code because of your thick fingers? How would you feel if he said you're too big to learn how to dance or do yoga? You have to think with more than your head. I know you want to protect him, but you can't always, and he has to learn. If he doesn't learn now, it'll be too late. Don't tear him down. Build him up and let him learn in his own time. You weren't a blackbelt or top of your platoon in hand-to-hand when you just started out. But think about when your dad tore you down. Think about how you felt. A man you looked up to. Someone you respected. I'm not saying it's the same, but it's similar. No one deserves to be treated as an inferior by their equal." Callum took the towel he had slung over a railing and wiped his face of perspiration. "I'm going to shower. Kiter wants to have a meeting as soon as everyone is up."

Vidar was silent during his speech but as he approached the door, Vidar spoke. "Captain America."

Callum turned. "What?"

"Tearing tree stumps in half with his bare hands was Captain America. Thor just would have struck them with lightning."

Callum breathed a laugh. "Then be more like Thor, Thor." He called him by his codename. "A natural born leader, the god of thunder, a mastermind, and yeah, the hot one." He winked.

Vidar watched as Callum left the gym and let his words settle in his mind. He hadn't reacted the best to Boyd's attempts, but all he could think of was Sasha coming back and hurting him. He needed to show him the best way. And that meant shelving his fear and possible arrogance and helping his friend, teammate, and the man who worked him up every time he saw him. He had to figure out the best way about it. And it wasn't critique. Maybe

Callum was right, he never wanted to be like his father... *so stop acting like him.*

Chapter Two

"I want the record to note that if this goes off without a hitch, I will be the greatest of all time," Boyd announced from beside Nigel's hospital bed. They had converted one of the rooms into a makeshift hospital and his friend and teammate, Nigel Sweet lay in the bed, casts on both legs, a compression cast on his torso, and an IV in his arm after the shooting and car accident caused by Sasha a week ago. But he had just woken up earlier that day.

Nigel chuckled from beneath the thin blanket as his fiancé Gabe Collins held his hand. "You want a little trophy?" He teased.

"That'd be nice," Boyd answered.

"I still don't like the idea," Kiter stated. "There's got to be another way."

"Don't you think I've tried?" Marjorie, their team admin, asked. "It's impenetrable. Ever since Hannah died I've tried." She looked down at the mention of her late wife. Boyd took her hand in his. He had no experience losing a spouse, but Marjorie's pain was vivid on her face.

"Breaking into a high-tech government vault secured by guards, cameras, infrared, and god only knows what else, is idiotic," Vidar stood and began pacing. "Let alone a suicide mission going against our own government."

"Awe Thor, I'm touched. It sounds like you almost care about me," Boyd said.

"You know I do, and I don't want you to do this," he stated.

"I don't recall asking your permission or needing it," Boyd replied, injecting ice into his tone.

"Dammit, you're not thinking clearly. You only see the prize, the title like a fucking carrot on a stick. You need to think rationally."

"So I'm an irrational dog now?"

"That's not—"

"You also missed highly skilled, a field agent, and gorgeous, but that might just be how I think of myself."

"Boyd, if you would just listen—"

"I'm deaf now too? You've made your position very clear, Agent Jørgensen. But allow me to make my own decisions. Now," Boyd turned back to Marjorie, effectively dismissing him. "Talk to me. What's the style of lasers and infrared?"

Marjorie glanced up at Vidar but began speaking as Boyd ignored Gabe standing from Nigel's hospital bed and walking over to Vidar. Boyd liked Vidar, he did. There was something about the sexy half-Norwegian-half-Swede that called to him. Thirty-six, six-foot-six, and muscled, he ticked all of Boyd's boxes. But the man was arrogant and self-deluded with his own sense of worth. And Boyd was afraid a little dalliance with him could get messy and Boyd didn't do messy. He was the king of one-night-stands and he liked it that way. It wasn't as if he didn't know the guy wanted him. And if he were honest he'd be happy to take a tumble between the sheets with him, but the problem was... he wasn't sure once would be enough and it scared the shit out of him. He didn't do relationships. Waking in the middle of the night screaming and having random panic attacks didn't bode well in the relationship department and he never spoke about it. Callum was the exception, having gone through something similar. Kiter knew and probably Rhys by default, but that was because of research and a little deduction.

He ignored Vidar and Gabe and focused on Marjorie and the plan. He wasn't lying when he said, if their plan to break into MI6's sub-basement top secret vault went off without a hitch, he would be the greatest of all time. And though he wouldn't mind a trophy, no one in the hacker or underground thief community could know. Still, the plan was making him giddy.

About twenty minutes later, at the doctor's urging Nigel to rest, all but Gabe left the room. Vidar was nowhere to be found and neither he nor Gabe had been seen since they left the planning room. Taking a deep breath, Boyd smelled the delicious foods Mama Sweet, Nigel's mother was making. The bunker was a safe house for the team and their families. Gabe's boys and his and Nigel's parents were there.

With Sasha on the loose, it was safer to have everyone they loved safe. But it also brought a pang of grief as Boyd had no one to protect. His parents died in a car accident when he was six and his grandpa had died of cancer when he was eight. There was no one else. Feeling the creeping sensation of the beginnings of a panic attack, he chose to focus on the beautiful Caribbean woman standing over the stove and grinned.

"Mama Sweet," he said saddling up to her side. "Good morning."

"Good morning, darlin'," she kissed his cheek, her wonderful accent caressing the words and making him smile. "Food will be ready in about thirty minutes."

"Smells amazing."

"Thank you, baby."

"Nigel's lucky to have grown up with you, Mama Sweet. I would have loved to be your son."

"You are, baby, all of you are. And I'm one proud mama."

His throat thickened unexpectedly. Instead of speaking and giving it away, he kissed her pudgy cheek and headed down the hall. He barely made it around the corner and out of sight of Nigel's dad watching the game with Gabe's father and sons before the emotions won out. He slapped his hand against the wall and bent to try to get a breath but couldn't. He opened his mouth, and his silent scream wracked his body. He couldn't get air into his lungs. He shook with another silent scream. The pain was overwhelming. Sometimes, he hated his parents. If they hadn't gone out that night to his dad's company Christmas party, they wouldn't have gotten stuck driving back in a blizzard. He wouldn't have lost them. He wouldn't have been forced to go to that horrible place to be used and abused by the evil men like the warden. He had gotten his revenge on him, but it wasn't enough. He would never forget. He would never be able to escape the thought swirling around his head, and he silently screamed again and let the tears, snot, and drool fall to the floor quietly.

Then, someone appeared behind him. Someone pulled him up. His back connected to a wide chest as arms came around him. He rested his head against the person's collarbone and panted through the pain. He was safe. He was loved. He was protected. And the shadows and demons scurried back into their dark holes in his mind.

"I'm sorry," he finally got out, though it was barely audible. He turned around and buried his head into the man's chest.

"Shh shh," the soothing voice said. He knew who it was, he could smell their cologne. It was cologne he hated to admit he loved. Even though he knew he should, he couldn't force his body to pull away. "I'm sorry about earlier," the slightly Norwegian accent said. "I do care about you, Boyd. I don't think you're... all those things you think I meant. And I'm sorry for how I reacted in the gym this morning. I'm scared. I want to be able to protect you and I feel like I can't. You don't want me to."

"It's not that. I'm your equal, Vidar," Boyd said pulling back to look up at the handsome face and blue eyes, he longed to get lost in. "Not your lesser. You have skills, I have skills. They just aren't the same but that doesn't make me any less of an agent or a man. And Callum was helping me. I've never thrown a punch in my life, and he was showing me. I'm not the lightweight champion, I'm not even a schoolyard bully, but you made me feel like I was useless."

"That was never my intention," Vidar said stroking a soothing hand up and down his back. "I just kept seeing you trying to hit Sasha like that and how he would react. He'd destroy you before I could get to you. It made me see red and I needed you to do it right."

"Then teach me." Boyd looked up at him. Vidar stared. "Teach me how to do it correctly."

Vidar didn't say anything at first and it gave Boyd a chance to study him. He knew every part of his face; he had stared enough times to have memorized it. Vidar was so handsome. He was the type of man who aged beautifully and would still look good, maybe even more so, in twenty to thirty years with a full head of white hair. But he hoped he would never grow a beard. Such a jaw line deserved to be seen.

"You want me to help you?" Vidar asked incredulously and Boyd slipped his hands up around his waist and rested his head on his chest.

"Yes. I need you to help me. Will you?"

"Of course."

Chapter

Three

A week had passed since their plan to break into the vault was put in place and every day they trained. In the morning, before everyone, apart from Callum, was awake, Boyd and Vidar met in the gym and Vidar taught him the proper way to punch and kick for his size. Boyd was strong and fit for his stature and Vidar enjoyed their training. But that day, he watched Boyd from the observation deck of their simulator which they built to the schematics and scale of the building's blueprints. The vault was at the end of the long winding corridor of Sub-Basement (SB) 9, MI6 Headquarters, with hallways where the guards patrolled. Rhys, Callum, Gabe, and Kiter posed as the guards with laser guns instead of real bullets and just like in American Laser Tag, they all wore vests with sensors to see if they would be shot in the real scenario. The infrared sensors – their training version at least – were added in the correct locations. The red-light alarm would go off signaling he was discovered and effectively the mission was a failure.

So far, red was Vidar's least favorite color.

Having experience in getting in and out of tight spaces in the SRR division of His Majesty's Special Forces,, Vidar stayed in the observation desk with a full view of the room and posed as Mission Control watching Boyd's every move.

"Autolycus, more lasers at your two and ten," he called to Boyd through their comms.

"I know," he whispered, breathing heavily after the acrobatics he had done to pass through the lasers.

"Calm your breathing. Infrared can pick up your breath's heat sig."

"Shut up and let me think."

The more times Boyd failed, the harsher he became. Vidar didn't take it personally; he'd been in his shoes. He knew the pressure he was under. Vidar watched as Boyd slipped down the wall and contorted his body over and under the lasers. He moved with the agility of a cat and the grace of a dancer. Vidar was mesmerized until he saw Rhys pacing in an unusual spot just around the corner. The rest of the team didn't have comms, so they didn't know where Boyd was and had a set location to patrol. But sometimes, they liked to switch things up to keep Boyd guessing as he would be during the real thing.

"Bogey, hold position."

Boyd froze. He was bent over backwards over a laser. "You've got to be kidding me."

"Hold your position, Autolycus."

Boyd steadied his breathing and held. Rhys walked back about ten seconds later. "Proceed slowly," Vidar said.

"What do you think I've been doing?" Boyd snarked. Nigel Sweet chuckled beside Vidar as he took in the scenario.

"Long day?" He asked seated in his wheelchair, both legs still in casts.

"He's yet to get it right all week," Vidar said not taking his eyes off the sim.

"That's not good for our Boyd."

"Yeah," Vidar stated, his eyes on Boyd as he passed the third laser location and approached more infrared cameras. Vidar's eyes bounced around the scene. "Two guards behind you, well done."

"Yeah yeah," Boyd said sounding exasperated.

Vidar felt Sweet's eyes on him, but he dared not look over. "What?"

"Nothing."

"Not nothing. What?"

Sweet huffed. "Well, I'm just wondering how everything is going. You two seem to be spending a lot more time together but still fighting the pull between you two."

"We're colleagues, nothing more. I'm training him."

"Bullshit."

"Sweet," he huffed, eyes still on Boyd. "Do I care for him? Yes, but he doesn't want me like that and I..."

"Don't tell me you're getting cold feet."

"I'm just not sure. He doesn't want to be my experiment and I wouldn't want to hurt him."

"Have you ever kissed a man?" Sweet asked.

Vidar's jaw clenched. "Yes, when Kiter and I went to that company party, I kissed him."

"That's different. That was fake. I'm talking about kissing a man you are actually attracted to."

"...No."

"So Kiter at that party is the full extent of your man loving?"

"Man loving?"

"You don't know if you're a top or bottom, a Daddy or a Dom, a cuddler or a loner?"

Vidar took a deep breath. "I've never done this before and even with women, sex wasn't the first thing on my mind. The first thing was hiding my sexuality from my father. Being with women always seemed like a chore. Something to prove to him I wasn't a fairy, as he called it."

"So even sex with women was unsatisfying?"

"I was satisfied," Vidar shrugged. "But it wasn't the whole fireworks thing everyone always talks about."

Sweet was quiet for a while before chuckling. "Oh my sweet little killing machine," he teased. "You're in for the ride of your life."

Unable to answer as Boyd approached the infrared, Vidar leaned forward and pressed the comm. "Autolycus, watch your heat sig—" Vidar couldn't get it out before the red alert hit.

"Goddammit!" Boyd shouted and Vidar winced as his earpiece rang.

"Uh oh," Sweet muttered.

Vidar didn't reply as he watched Boyd punch the wall and stalk away. Without another word, Vidar left and followed Boyd's path to the dressing room. He heard him before he saw him. Boyd was slamming locker doors and cursing like a sailor. Vidar let him continue for a few more seconds before he entered the room. The team came up behind him, but he held a hand silently asking for a moment alone. Rhys nodded and held the rest of the team back.

Walking in, he stood, feet apart, arms crossed over his large chest and stared at him. "Well, that was a shit show."

"Where were you? You could have told me sooner," Boyd demanded stalking over to him.

"Contrary to your belief, I was monitoring everything, but it took less than two seconds for your body heat to be detected. What would you have done in two seconds?"

"Plenty," he replied.

"You're deluding yourself," Vidar supplied. "This isn't working, you know it. I know it. The whole team knows it. So what are we going to do, huh? Throw a little temper tantrum like a toddler? Or are we going to put our heads together and figure out another way?"

"Fuck you, I'm not having a temper tantrum."

"Really?" Vidar was unconvinced. "So what do you call this then? An exercise in diplomacy? You want the team to stop treating you like the youngest member, then stop acting like it."

"Sod off!"

"Oh yes, very mature," he answered.

Boyd let out a roar and raced to him. Vidar held his arms by the wrist as Boyd struggled to reach him. Though Boyd was strong, he was no match for Vidar's bulk. Even after a week of training, Boyd still fought with his emotions and not with his head like Vidar was teaching him.

"Ugh! I hate you!" Boyd yelled.

"No you don't," Rhys' voice came next. "And he's right, you

know." Without warning, Rhys grabbed Boyd around the middle and slung him over his shoulder in a fireman's hold.

"Put me down!" Boyd shouted. Rhys slapped Boyd's ass, hard, and the man squealed in anger. "What does your *husband* think of you spanking your former one-night stand lover?" Boyd spat.

"I think it's hilarious," Kiter answered, and they all followed Rhys down the hall, hearing Boyd's constant shouts of indignation.

It took Vidar a minute to figure out where they were headed.

"What are you doing?" Boyd shouted seeing the pool behind him. "Put me down!"

"With pleasure," Rhys answered and unceremoniously dropped him into the pool.

Boyd surfaced a few seconds later, sputtering and coughing. He looked up at Rhys and the team and let out a feral shout.

"You're going to act like a child, you'll get treated as one," Rhys said.

"I am *not* a child!"

"Then stop throwing a tantrum," Kiter said. "Now, we're going back in there and doing this again, but this time Vidar is going in with you."

"What?" Vidar questioned.

"I don't need his help! I can do this!"

"No, you can't," Kiter said. "As proven seven times over. I refuse to allow this pure definition of insanity to continue. Vidar goes in with you this time and you will listen to him, or I am pulling the plug on this whole thing."

"You can't do that!" Boyd argued.

"Try me," Kiter threatened. "Get dried off and get back to the sim. You have five minutes." With that, Kiter, Rhys, Callum, and Gabe left the pool. Vidar stood at the edge.

Boyd let out a grunt and looked up at Vidar. "Don't," he spat.

Vidar crouched at the side of the pool. "I know you're used to doing things on your own," he kept his voice soft. "But you're not alone anymore. Let me help."

Boyd stared up at him, his hair shining, soaking wet. His face glowed with the aftereffects of anger. His perfect bow lips pursed, and his beautiful eyes closed for a moment. When he finally looked up at him, he let out a sigh. "Fine. Sorry for the outburst," he muttered.

The tip of Vidar's lip ticked up. "Don't worry about it. We've all been there." Vidar offered his hand and Boyd waded through the water to the steps and accepted his help. "Go get dry and I'll meet you at the sim. We'll get this. I promise."

Chapter Four

With a clearer head, Boyd walked into the simulation room, stopping short when he saw Vidar. Decked out in tactical gear, he looked intimidating, but Boyd couldn't help the bit of drool that escaped his mouth. Vidar wore a grey green long sleeved shirt with their modified laser tag vests. His belt was secured around his hips and had three modified laser guns, a retractable tactical knife, and a paint taser. His upper arm had the comm receiver and his codename was Velcroed to the vest. But what made Boyd swallow hard and caused his pants to tighten a bit were the two leg straps holding two more guns and a diving knife surrounding his upper thigh. The straps cradled between the creases of his thighs and enhanced his rather... large bulge between his legs. He was adjusting the straps and himself to get more comfortable when he looked up and froze.

"Damn," Boyd finally said. "Our boy is packin'."

Vidar's eyes grew large at the connotation and when he heard Rhys chuckle, Boyd added. "When do I get a gun?"

"Never," Kiter answered.

"No fair," Boyd pouted then turned a salacious grin to Vidar. "Guess I'll just have to play with yours, Thor." He winked and walked over to him. If he put a little more swing in his hips, so be it.

"Stay behind me," Vidar told him gruffly when Kiter announced they were ready. "Disable the infrared before we get there."

"All well and good in theory, but how exactly? The control panel is on the opposite side."

"Use every asset at your disposal." Vidar glanced up at the observational desk where Sweet was watching still seated in his wheelchair.

"Why didn't you tell me that before?" Boyd questioned.

"Because I wasn't in the sim with you," Vidar replied. "You wanted to do it all yourself."

"Okay okay," Boyd waved him off and pressed his finger to his ear comm. "Diamond, come in?" Boyd called to Sweet.

"Go ahead," Sweet answered.

"I need you to hack into the building schematic and disable the infrared."

"Ehum, I'm not..."

"I'll walk you through it," Boyd promised. "The back door I set up earlier should be there. Find the file on the desktop named *Deus ex Machina.*"

Vidar gave him a look and Boyd shrugged, beaming as Vidar's eye roll. "Check," Sweet said over their comms.

"Now hit F7, that will launch the program."

"Whoa," Sweet replied.

Boyd loved showing his skills to luddites. "Now find something named TIIF."

"TIIF confirmed."

"Click and once it opens, you'll see the thermal infrared camera images, confirm?"

"Affirmative."

"I need you to type exactly what I tell you," Boyd tapped Vidar on the shoulder and gave him a thumbs up. Vidar nodded and pressed the button on the wall indicating they were starting the sim. With a hand on Vidar's shoulder, Boyd followed through the hallways of the sim while whispering to Sweet. "Romeo, Alpha, Juliet, Lima, Oscar, 6-1-4-7-7-0, Uniform, Bravo, over."

"Confirmed."

"On my mark, F11."

"Understood," Sweet said.

Vidar held up his fist telling them to stop. After a beat, his fist opened to a flat palm and Boyd stayed put as Vidar stepped forward quickly and pulled the trigger on his laser gun. Then, he waved Boyd forward. Boyd glanced down the hallway to see Gabe standing, watching them, an unhappy look on his face as his hands rested on his hips. Boyd gave him a smirk and a little wave. Gabe and Vidar had been in friendly competition since Vidar arrived. They both were sharpshooters and Gabe was very competitive.

Boyd followed Vidar down another hallway, then another. Vidar held his gun in a ready stance like Boyd had seen in military movies. Vidar stopped again, holding up his fist, seemingly waiting for the *guard* to pass. Once he did, Vidar motioned with two fingers for Boyd to follow. He did. They reached the laser area. The red lights dancing as they scanned the area. Vidar motioned him forward.

"Turn off switch is on the opposite wall," Boyd whispered. "I'll hit it once I'm through."

"The hack code won't shut this down?" Vidar questioned.

"It would but it also would alert HQ we're here. I'd rather wait until the last second."

"Understood. Be careful," Vidar took the messenger bag that Boyd carried and stepped back, watching.

Boyd nodded once and turned to the lights. They were harmless in the sim but Boyd still took a deep breath as if they could cut in him two, centered his mind. Letting his body fall forward, he tucked and rolled. Standing, he curled his torso back as one light swung his way and he let his momentum carry him backwards into a Hollow Back handstand. His arms straight, neck lengthened, chest forward, shoulders together, hips perpendicular to his rib cage, legs up and together. He breathed slowly. Once the laser passed over him, he lowered his legs into a full split and tucked his body under another laser while bringing his right leg behind him and left leg in front in an S position. His torso moved in a circle following one of the lasers. Tucking into a roll, he pulled up into a handstand and lowered his body over the final laser. Taking a second to catch his breath, he reached for the switch and turned off the lasers. Vidar hurried through the corridor, cheeks red and his lower area much more pronounced.

"Damn," Vidar breathed. Boyd grinned but said nothing more as he followed Vidar down the hall.

Callum appeared in front of them as surprised to see them

as they were. Before Callum could call out, Vidar grabbed him and slipped his arm around Callum's throat, not squeezing like he would in a real fight, but Boyd saw Callum play along. Vidar pulled out his retractable knife and "stabbed" Callum in the neck and chest before Boyd could even blink. Callum slipped to the floor and nodded to Boyd. Vidar and Boyd continued on down the hallway. They only had two more hallways to go. Boyd followed Vidar without question. They didn't run into either Rhys or Kiter as they reached the infrared.

"Diamond," Boyd said and squeezed Vidar's shoulder to stop him.

"Go," they heard Sweet say.

"F11, now," Boyd ordered.

"Affirmative, cameras are down," Sweet said.

A small red light appeared over the room.

"They know we're here. Three minutes tops," Boyd told Vidar.

"Go," Vidar ordered. "I'll cover you." He handed him the messenger bag.

Boyd nodded once and raced to the heavy vault door. Hacking the code, he grinned at the sound of the locks sliding back. He spun the spindle lock and pulled the door open.

"FCEE290717," he muttered to himself scanning the different vaults that looked like safety deposit boxes.

"Ninety seconds, Autolycus," Vidar said.

"Confirmed, I'm looking." His eyes found the vault. "Eyes on the prize."

"Get it and let's go. Two guards already taken out," Vidar grunted.

"You say the sexiest things," he teased.

"Move your ass, Auto."

"Again, you say the sexiest things," he said as he opened the vault. He didn't stop to look, he just grabbed the stack of papers, cassette tapes, and laptop computer stuffing everything into his bag. Without knowing what to expect in the real vault, they added meaningless things from the storage room in their offices.

"Auto!"

"Done, let's go," he said as he rushed to Vidar's side. He fired his laser gun at Gabe who, pretending to be another officer, dropped. Rhys was directly behind him, and Vidar didn't hesitate.

"Get behind me," Vidar ordered. Kiter and Callum rushed them and fired at them. Vidar ducked and returned fire.

Boyd held onto his vest as they raced back through the maze. Vidar took out Rhys again, then Callum.

"Thor!" Boyd yelled seeing Gabe and Kiter come up behind him.

Vidar turned smoothly and fired but not before Gabe fired back.

"I'm hit," Vidar called seeing one of the laser lights on his vest light up. "Go," he handed Boyd his side arm. Boyd hesitated. "Go!" Vidar shouted and Boyd ran.

Rhys appeared in front of him. He fired. Rhys went down. Kiter was next. Boyd fired.

The Mission Accomplished button was in sight. Boyd would be damned if he didn't hit it that time.

Gabe stepped in front of the button and raised his gun. Boyd ducked and rolled, then fired. Gabe went down. With a shout of eureka, Boyd lunged for the button and slapped his hand down. The green lights showed throughout the sim room and Boyd squealed.

The team sauntered out of the maze, and he launched himself at Vidar who caught him with a surprised grunt.

"That was incredible!" Boyd gushed.

"Yes, even though your partner was killed," Kiter chuckled.

"Mission accomplished, right?" Boyd questioned.

"Ooh harsh," Rhys winked.

"With friends like that, Vi, who needs enemies?" Callum teased.

"Oh shut it," Boyd grinned then looked up at Vidar. "I would have mourned you, Thor."

"How generous of you," Vidar replied.

"Mama says food's ready, boys," Sweet called over the intercom.

"Oh sweet baby Jesus, thank god!" Boyd said. "I'm starving."

"You're always starving, kid," Rhys said.

"You know what it takes to do the acrobatics I pulled off in there?" He questioned, then grinned when he saw Vidar subtly adjusted himself. "Was that hot, Baby Thor? Did you like seeing me... flexible?"

Vidar's face turned bright red, and he looked away.

"Stop teasing him, Boyd," Rhys said.

"Oh, but it's so fun."

"Sadist," Gabe called.

"Proud one too," Boyd teased.

They all headed up to the observation room where Sweet sat in his wheelchair. His fiancé walked over to him, bending to give him a kiss.

"Did you see me?" Gabe asked.

Nigel chuckled. "Yes, baby, I saw you. You were hot all commanding and shit." Gabe grinned then took the handles of Sweet's wheelchair and turned him to the main living room.

"You all go ahead," Vidar said. "I'm going to shower."

"We'll save you a plate," Gabe promised.

"Cheers," and he pushed open the door leading to the dressing room. Boyd hesitated wanting to go with him to thank him, but decided to wait and followed the rest of the team. The spot beside him was empty and cold without Vi. Trusting Vidar so implicitly through the sim, messed with his head. *That's all it is.* Anyone would feel that way. Though it was fake, and the bad guys were his teammates, he still felt a strong connection with Vidar as they accomplished their mission. And when he went down, hit by the laser gun, Boyd had a moment of panic and fear until he reminded himself it wasn't real. Still. The idea of Vidar getting hurt, he shook his head. *No, he can't. I won't allow it.*

Seeing Boyd do all his acrobatics, Hollow Back handstands, and splits, to get past the lasers, made Vidar instantly hard. Boyd's lithe body, like a dancer, moving and contorting in such a way that all Vidar could see was him naked and in his bed. He was happy his pants were loose enough to conceal his erection but when Boyd launched himself at him, embracing him with those strong arms, a bright smile on his flawless face, Vidar needed a moment alone.

As the hot water pummeled his chest, his erection wouldn't subside. He was perpetually aroused ever since he started on the team. And as he took himself in hand, stroking in time to a fantasy in his head, he had to scoff. He'd jerked off in the showers more than ever before, but it wasn't like he had time to date let alone get laid. He guessed he could hook up, but the thought of meaningless sex never appealed to him. It had been too long, that was all.

He slapped his hand against the tile of the shower stall as he came on a grunt. At least his orgasm took a little longer that time. The first time he had wanked at the thought of Boyd, he had come embarrassingly fast just picturing his face with those sinful pouty lips.

Coming down quickly from his climax, he washed his body and hair efficiently, rinsed, and grabbed the towel he had hooked on the wall. Wiping his face, he wrapped the white towel around his waist and pulled back the curtain. Walking back to the main area of the dressing room, he came to an abrupt stop when he saw Callum standing there.

"Didn't want to interrupt," he said, and Vidar felt his cheeks heat. He'd been caught wanking in the showers so many times before in the army and in the SRR. Hell, he'd walked in on his best friends going at it and never did he ever blush, but for some reason, the thought of Callum hearing him, made blood stain and heat his cheeks.

Callum chuckled. "Don't worry about it. I've seen him do yoga. That boy is flexible. It's only a natural reaction. No judgment."

"Sorry," Vidar mumbled.

"Forget it," Callum said. "I was just washing up for dinner but didn't want to the kind of guy who heard you and left. Figured it was better to let you know, however embarrassing."

Vidar swallowed. "Thanks." Though he probably would have preferred not to never know Callum knew.

"Get dressed. You know he's going to eat everything."

Nodding dumbly, Vidar watched him go and quickly dressed. He tried to force his embarrassment to subside as he left the dressing room, but it wouldn't budge. As he walked into the main living area, the smells of Caribbean cooking surrounded him.

"So, when are we doing this?" Boyd questioned around a mouthful of corn bread as Vidar sat in the seat beside Boyd.

"Do what?" One of Gabe's sons questioned at the table.

"Daddy's work, Colton," Gabe winked.

"Oh," the little boy bounced.

"Well," Kiter began. "You've only successfully run the sim once and I'd say that was only about seventy percent successful since you know what happened." Kiter was ever tactful with young ears and civilians around. "So, we'll run it a few more times and when I'm confident it can go off without a hitch, we'll plan more."

"Oh come on," Boyd groaned. "I'm going stir crazy over here, boss. I got to do something."

"Your laundry is piling up," Rhys offered. Boyd stuck his tongue out at his friend. "Oh very mature," Rhys continued. The team chuckled and Boyd tossed a bit of cornbread at Rhys.

"Now boys," Gabe looked at his sons. "Do not follow any of Uncle Boyd's bad habits, understand?" Then, Gabe's eyes met Boyd's. "We don't throw food at the dinner table."

"Yes, Daddy," Gabe's boys and Boyd said at the same time.

"Daddy," the youngest, Colton, tugged on Gabe's sleeve. "Why did Uncle Boyd call you Daddy? You're not his dad."

Nigel coughed, choking on his water. Gabe's face pinked as he let out an exasperated sigh. "Because your Uncle Boyd is immature and incorrigible."

"What's incorrigible?" Hunter asked.

"It means he's a bit of a hellion," Gabe's dad said with a chuckle.

"I want to be incorrigible!" Colton said bouncing in his chair.

"You already are," Nigel winked at his fiancé's son and Colton beamed.

"Look," Kiter began, changing the subject. "I know we're all antsy. We all want to go home but this is the safest place for us all right now. It's not for long, I promise. But until we are assured of our families' safety, let's keep things amenable."

"We don't mind one bit," Nigel's dad spoke up. The man's sheer size dwarfed everyone in the room, but he was a teddy bear, especially with the two little boys in their midst. "It feels like vacation."

"So long as you don't mind us using the pool to keep the boys entertained," Gabe's dad said. "We're good."

"Of course, always," Kiter replied. "And Mrs. Sweet, this food is just amazing."

"So glad you like it, darlin'," she beamed.

"You're going to spoil us," Rhys said. "Maybe I should make my lasagna just to bring everyone's expectations down." He looked pointedly at his husband.

"Babe, you know I love your cooking. That better not be directed at me," Kiter winked.

"It's the least I can do for you taking care of my baby," Mrs. Sweet said reaching for Nigel's hand.

"Baby? Mama, I'm thirty-three," Nigel replied.

"Still and will always be my baby," she cupped his face.

"Has the doctor said how you're healing, Nigel?" Callum

asked.

"Average," he shrugged. "It's only been a couple weeks, but he seems happy with how things are progressing."

"Good," Callum nodded.

Before anyone else spoke, Vidar's phone rang, and he smiled at the ringtone. Pushing back from the table, he looked at Mrs. Sweet. "Forgive me, I have to take this. I'll be right back."

"Of course, love," she waved him off.

Hurrying down the hallway, he shut the door to his room and answered the video call. "Hey, baby," he sighed.

Chapter Five

Boyd flopped belly down on his bed and pulled out his phone. He hadn't checked social media for a while, not that he showed his real identity. According to TikTok and Insta, he was a twenty-one-year-old white cis female living in South Hampton who liked Miley Cyrus, makeup, comedy, and dance. Most of it was true.

Opening Insta, he saw a new video from his favorite gay makeup artist and clicked on it. The man looked beautiful with his purple and pink eyeshadow, flawless complexion, and striking eyes. His newest comedy sketch had Boyd laughing so hard tears escaped but he definitely wanted to try to recreate the man's look. After the third time watching the short sketch, he screenshot a picture and pulled it up on his photos. Stripping out of his shirt, he set the phone down on the desk he had transitioned into his makeup station. It was a hobby and he'd only done full drag twice in his life, but he loved it and with his features, he made a very convincing woman. Turning on his Miley Cyrus playlist, he sat at the desk and pulled out his makeup kit.

He was just applying eyeliner when he heard Vidar's faint voice through the wall. He stopped and listened, but it wasn't loud enough for him to make out more than two or three words. Curious, and unsure why, he stood and pressed his ear to the wall. The muffled voice became slightly less muffled, and he could hear him.

"...sure she's... there's more in... I miss you too, baby."

Whoa! What? Boyd reared back. Vidar had a... *baby?* Is it a man or a woman... or was he a father? Why hadn't he said anything? Leaning forward again, Boyd heard more.

"...talk to the boss and... home soon... before... I need to... okay, see you soon." Then, his voice went quiet.

What the hell? Boyd's jaw tightened and he ignored the knots in his stomach. Part of him wanted to march next door and demand an explanation, but another part wasn't sure he wanted to know. So, he sat back at his desk and stared unseeing at his reflection.

Vidar has a partner? Why didn't he say? Who is it? And why did the idea cause Boyd's stomach to twist?

He couldn't possibly be jealous. *No,* Boyd shook his head. *Absolutely not.* There was no way. But... then why did he feel so shitty? Huffing a sigh, he pulled himself out of his desk chair and grabbed his holdall. He needed to go home. He wanted to check on his plant babies and get fresh clothes. Rhys was right, his laundry was piling up. It wasn't that he was lazy, he was just used to having more clothes to choose from and only did a large load when he desperately needed clean clothes.

Heading out of his room, he found his boss having a cup of coffee with his husband.

"Nice," Kiter smiled when he saw him and only then did Boyd remember he was wearing full face makeup. He wasn't embarrassed, why would he be? But he hadn't told his team of his obsession yet. They had only seen him with matte foundation and eyeliner.

"Like it?" He asked, his sassiness coming out like a shield. "I followed my favorite makeup artist."

"Looks very nice," Rhys nodded.

"What's with the holdall?" Kiter asked eyes dropping to the bag in his hand.

"I need to head home, get more clothes and shit."

Kiter and Rhys nodded slowly. "Just be careful and aware."

"Yeah, 'course," Boyd replied.

"All right," Kiter agreed. "We want to run through the sim again. If you could be back tomorrow morning, that'd be great."

Boyd smiled. "Thanks boss, I'll be here."

Kiter nodded once then headed to the living room as Gabe's boys pulled out a board game. "Ah ha!" Kiter teased them. "Whatcha go there, lads?"

"Come play with us, Uncle Somm!" Colton cried excitedly.

"You boys are going to be too good to play against. I'll lose every time."

"There's no winners or losers in the Game of Life, Uncle Somm," Hunter stated pulling the box lid off the game.

"Wise beyond your years, Hunt," Kiter winked.

Boyd pulled his eyes away from his boss as Kiter sat cross-legged on the floor next to Hunter. He looked over at Rhys whose soft eyes were on his husband, but soon turned to Boyd and placed a hand on his shoulder.

"You all right?" He asked.

Boyd nodded and forced a smile. Rhys was the one he was closest to besides Callum and even though they'd had a one-night stand long ago, he looked at him more as a best friend or a brother. "Just something on my mind."

"Anything you want to talk about? Get it off your chest?" Rhys asked.

"Not really. Still not happy you got married without me, though." He may have meant it as a joke, but deep down he was a little hurt.

Rhys' face pinched in a wince. "I'm sorry. It wasn't intentional. Honestly, it was a spur of the moment thing. I thought he was joking when he proposed. Then, we just decided we wanted to keep it a secret especially after Gabe's wife did what she did. We didn't want to rub his face in it."

"But..." Boyd cursed the lump in his throat. "It's me."

Rhys pulled him into a hug and crushed the breath out of him. "I'm so sorry, Boyd. I didn't think you'd be so upset. Hey, listen," he pulled back and looked at him. "We're thinking about having a reception. Plan it for us?"

"Really?" His eyes brightened.

"Really. Just promise me you'll take our tastes into consideration. No inflatable cocks."

"No fair," he winked. "Tasteful... dull... boring... got it."

"Hey," Rhys teased, then went serious. "We have to get this mission done first and don't want to step on Gabe's and Nigel's planning, so coordinate?"

"Deal," Boyd beamed.

"Good. Now, be safe. Let me know when you get home."

"Yes, Daddy," Boyd rolled his eyes. "I am twenty-one, you know."

"You wouldn't do the same for me?" Rhys called his bluff.

"I guess," he begrudgingly agreed.

"Get outta here," Rhys chuckled.

Boyd laughed and stepped around him heading to the door.

"Boyd," Rhys called him back. He turned. "Your makeup really does look good. Really brings out your eyes."

Boyd refused to let the tears fill his eyes. He wasn't used to people complimenting him and Rhys' warmth touched his heart.

"I look good in anything," was all he could get out before he turned and swallowed the emotion threatening to escape.

He wasn't usually emotional and hated the, what he classified as, weakness. His mind raced with the possible reason why he was so weepy. He froze as his thumb punched the button for the garage.

It was the nineteenth. The day his grandpa died. His lips went a little tingly and his palms began to sweat. How could he have forgotten? So much going on in his life. No matter what he did in the past, he always remembered.

Almost in a trance, he reached the garage and found his car. It was a luxury he wasn't used to. He never had his own car until a couple weeks ago when Kiter mentioned his brother was wanting to sell his old Honda. He drove on autopilot toward the cemetery stopping to get a couple bouquets of flowers from the petrol station on his way. His parents were buried in the same cemetery near his grandpa.

Finding a place to park, he grabbed the flowers and got out of the car. He shocked himself seeing his reflection in the window. He'd forgotten about his makeup. No wonder he had gotten odd and dirty looks at the petrol station. Closing his eyes for a moment, he took a breath and then turned and walked across the cemetery toward his family's plots.

He stopped first at his grandpa's grave.

"Hey, Papa," he said softly as he laid the flowers at his gravestone. "I'm sorry I haven't been around recently. I got a new job. A good one. I hope you're proud of me. I got some good friends too. You'd like Rhys and Kiter. They're military like you. And... Vidar. He's Special Forces, or — I mean — I guess they all were. But... Vidar's special. Papa, I don't do relationships but ever since I met him, I've... wanted more."

Then why do you fill your life with those who waste your time? He felt his grandpa's voice and heaved a sigh.

"I'm... scared," he admitted.

Of?

"Losing him like I lose everyone I care about."

Oh my boy, he felt his grandpa's hand cup his cheek. *You can't live your life worrying about losing someone. That's not living. Your life will pass you by and you'll have regrets. Now, what did I always tell you?*

"No regrets," Boyd said.

That's right. Now, go say hello to your mother, it's too cold to be out for long.

"Yes, sir," and with that, Boyd got up, kissed his fingers and pressed them against his grandfather's headstone then walked toward his parent's graves.

Vidar hung up the phone and popped his head out of his room hearing his boss's voice cry out in what sounded like playful exclamation. He smiled softly when he saw his boss playing a board game with Gabe's sons. He hated to interrupt but he needed to. Kiter looked up and saw him. Vidar motioned for him to come over. Kiter excused himself from the game and headed to Vidar.

"What's up?" he asked when he stepped into the room.

"I was hoping it would be all right to head home for a couple hours. There's something I need to check on."

"Sure, yeah. Boyd already left. Just be aware and safe."

"Boyd left?" Vidar asked.

"Yeah," Kiter answered, an odd look in his eye. "Needed to go home. I'll tell you what I told him. Try to be back by tomorrow morning?"

"Yeah, good, I can do that."

"Good, have fun."

Vidar said nothing more and hurried to the lift. He had never been so eager to get home. Not even when he had been deployed. He merely wanted to get home and bask in *her* love. The love only *she* could give. He missed her so much. They hadn't been apart that long in years. But as he got to his car, he found himself turning right instead of left at the exit. Unsure why he was doing what he was doing, he let it go, and pulled up at the apartment complex he'd never been to but knew well. He stared at the old white building in a moderate area of town. It was one of those retro places easily converted into a high rise of fourteen stories. Kids played in a small field across the way and a young father walked with his toddler down the overgrown cracked sidewalk. What had drawn him there, Vidar was afraid to answer, but he popped the door of his SUV and headed to the front. Palms sweaty as he reached for the buzzer, he nearly jumped back when the door opened. A young woman was struggling to maneuver a pram and Vidar clasped the edge of the door.

"Can I help?" he offered.

"Oh, ta," she smiled. It took less than twenty seconds but to Vidar, stomach in knots, cold sweat trickling down his back, it took much longer.

With a wave, the woman left him holding the door. He debated going in as a fly buzzed by his face. The annoying insect flew inside and danced down the hall, its small wings carrying it to its almost certain doom. A robin landed on the pale cement in front of him, its nimble yellow beak pecking at an abandoned piece of fried potato. *Oh to be that bird. Without a care.* But instead, with a breath of promise and reserved terrifying joy, Vidar took that step and the door slammed shut behind him, bathing him in the muted light of his new life.

His eyes drew down the hallway. It was dimly lit and stretched on forever and the faint strains of music drifted out into the afternoon sky.

Finding Boyd's flat was easy, even if he didn't know the number. Once on the top floor, he followed the music; a pounding base that grew louder and louder with every step he took. Boyd's door was marked with the number 1401. He gathered his courage and knocked.

The music softened after a brief moment and the bolt slid back. "What are you doing here?" Boyd questioned when he swung the door open.

Vidar's eyes drew down to his chest, glistening with sweat and... *is that glitter?*

"Vi? Vidar," Boyd's voice caught his attention, and he looked up. The man's eyes were vibrant as his chest heaved.

"I... should have called. I didn't mean to... interrupt." He turned and paced back to the lift.

In a daze, he pushed the call button and waited. *Stupid, so stupid.* He berated himself. He should have known Boyd was entertaining. He really didn't need to see it... again. A soft hand on his shoulder made him jerk his head.

Boyd stood behind him, still wearing nothing but tight black shorts. "You didn't answer my question," he began. "What are you doing here?"

"Nothing, it was stupid."

"Shouldn't you let me figure that out?"

"I don't want to interrupt. You look like you have company."

"And you're... jealous? Angry?"

Yes and yes, he thought. "Neither." Lying always came easy to him. It was a wonderful technique to have in the Special Forces, but it left a foul taste in his mouth as he spoke. Boyd pulled back and crossed his arms over his chest.

"Oh really?" he asked.

The lift doors dinged. "Really. Tell him, sorry for bothering you. I'll let you get back." Vidar stepped inside.

"Join us," he answered.

"What?" He turned to look at him.

"If you're so unbothered by it, join us."

"No, thank you. Threesomes are not my thing."

"It seems a lot is not your thing."

50

"I have standards."

"And I don't?" Boyd snapped.

Vidar huffed. "Look, I'm sorry I didn't call. I should have and I will never make that mistake again. I just wanted to check on you and I shouldn't have. Enjoy whatever his name is."

The brushed silver doors were closing. The musty scent of an overused lift filled his nose. He averted his eyes from Boyd's form as he slowly disappeared behind the doors. Closing his eyes, Vidar kicked himself. Again he had made the wrong decision, as usual. *Stupid. Stupid!*

The bang clattered through the small space and drew his stunned attention. Boyd's hand had shot out and stopped the lift doors from closing. The doors slowly slid back open, and Vidar was confronted with the bane of his desires.

"Exercise, dickhead."

"Excuse me?"

Boyd sighed harshly. "There is no guy. I was exercising. Now, you want to tell me what you're doing here?"

Vidar's brain finally caught up. "There's no guy?"

Boyd rolled his eyes and let out a harsh sigh. "I'm tempted to find one just so this all makes sense and takes up less time. Now, what the fuck are you doing here?"

"I... wanted to check on you. Kiter said you had left. I didn't know if you were... all right."

The lift doors began to shut again, and Boyd stopped them once more. "Could you get out of the lift please, so we can have a proper conversation?"

Vidar hesitated for a moment before stepping back onto Boyd's floor. Without words, he followed him down the hallway back to his flat. Once inside, the door shut behind him, he took in the space before him. The sprawling rooms spanned the entire building with exposed dark concrete beaming on the ceiling drawing his eyes up and around to the white walls and dark hardwood floors, a stark contrast. Columns lined the middle of the hallway separating the living areas and showcasing the built-in floor-to-ceiling bookshelves in one section of the wall. The classic artwork and modern sculptures complemented the area in a unique, unhurried way.

"This is beautiful," Vidar whispered.

"Thanks, it came with the building." Boyd stepped down the three small steps and crossed the open floorplan.

"What?" Vidar questioned following him.

Filling two glasses of water, Boyd walked back over to him. Still shirtless. Still covered in sweat and glitter.

"The flat. It came with the building," he clarified.

"You own the complex?"

Boyd nodded. "I... came into some money a few years ago."

There was a long pause as they drank the water. Awkwardness never fully leaving their sight. After chugging his drink, Boyd stared, and Vidar wasn't sure what he was looking for. A beat later, Boyd turned away and walked to the windows. Vidar felt the emptiness and watched him. Taking in the way his lean muscles moved under the expanse of skin, Vidar wanted nothing more than to slid his hands up and down the smooth skin.

Chapter Six

Boyd stared out the floor to ceiling window. Seeing Vidar on the other side of the door was a surprise, but his words hurt. He should have slammed the door in his face, not followed him out to the lift. But for some unknown reason, he needed Vidar to know he wasn't with a guy. It was none of his business.

But a part of him wanted to climb the Norwegian like a tree, the other wanted to give him a show and make him suffer. And yet another part of him wanted to kick him out of his home and lock the door behind him.

Tired of the cat and mouse game, he turned to Vidar, looking wholly uncomfortable in his space, and decided to do one of the scariest things he had ever done... and that included taking down the man who raped him. He stared Vidar and took one step closer. Instinctively, Vidar stepped back.

"Do you know what I was doing before you interrupted me?" His voice was low, and he found perverse pleasure in watching Vidar lick his lips and swallow convulsively.

"Exercise?" he offered and for such a large man to have his voice squeak was its own kind of adorable.

"Yes," Boyd agreed slowly walking over to him. "Would you like to know how I exercise?" Vidar stood frozen a step in front of the couch. He didn't flinch when Boyd slid his hands up Vidar's arms and down his chest. With a gentle nudge, Vidar fell, ass first on the sofa and Boyd held in his grin. "Do you want to see the exercise you interrupted?" His voice husky and his eyes hooded. He watched Vidar shiver then, after a moment's hesitation, nod emphatically. Boyd reveled in his success.

He pulled down the faux light switch in the wall and keyed in his code on the high-tech computer screen he'd installed. His own creation to rival the virtual assistants currently so popular online. Giving the command to lower the curtains, the natural light Boyd loved so much blacked out. Then, with an immense pride, he clicked on the music icon, queuing up his favorite workout song. He had paid extra to insulate his apartment. He was under no delusion it was soundproofed but he gave his tenants below him a discount on rent to compensate. Once Miley Cyrus' *Gimme What I Want* was ready, he programed the lights around the center column to produce a red hue, then clicked the X icon on the panel. The plaster casing of the column lowered into the ground revealing his pride and joy, a titanium gold dance pole. He peeked at Vidar sitting very straight, hands on his thighs, eyes wide with a mixture of fear and arousal. The corner of Boyd's lip tipped up.

Setting the timer for ten seconds, the lights switching off bathing them in complete darkness, he made his way to his pole and rested his back against it, his left hand rose above his head, and he wrapped his fingers around the cool metal, his right extended behind him and gripped the pole at the small of his back.

At the first sounds of the electric bass guitar filtering through the ceiling speakers, Boyd took a deep breath. As soon as the drums joined the guitar, the red lights came on and Boyd lost himself in Miley's voice.

Vidar was transfixed, mesmerized, spellbound. He couldn't move and he couldn't take his eyes off Boyd. The man was worshiping the pole and moving his body in ways Vi had never seen. He swung his legs up and around the pole, locking his feet around it and letting go with his hands. His body glistened in the red lighting. The music pulsed and the woman sang on the music track, but Vidar honestly could not hear the lyrics, only the pounding of his blood. His body reacted, his cock hardening behind the confines of his jeans but he couldn't move to adjust the ache.

Vidar wasn't sure how long the dance was, but Boyd eventually slid down the pole and slowly landed in a full split, his eyes on him. Boyd's chest heaved with his breaths, but Vidar stayed exactly where he was. He could not move, even if the building was burning down. He would have happily stayed watching Boyd and they would burn together. That thought roused him slightly. But when Boyd spoke, it wasn't to him.

"Hey, LOVE, bring up the lights to thirty percent." The living room illuminated automatically. "And raise the curtains to half."

Natural light flooded the floor as the blackout curtains lifted halfway. Boyd never dropped Vidar's gaze and after a beat, he stood smoothly swaying toward him. He stood directly over Vidar, their eyes locked. Vidar couldn't breathe after the performance, but the air in his lungs evaporated when Boyd knelt before him. His thin fingers and pale hands rested on his knees. Vidar stared at the elegant fingers as they began to move upwards. His knees, his thighs, his inner thighs. He jolted when Boyd's thumbs, feather light, touched his groin. His very pronounced, hard, and achy groin. Their eyes met.

"Did you like what you saw?" Boyd's voice was breathy. "Did you like seeing me dance for you? Worship the pole like I want to worship your cock?"

His thumbs continued their feather light touch on his balls through the rough material of his jeans as his eyes remained locked on Vidar's.

"I would, you know... worship it. I'd make you feel better than you ever felt before. Want me to show you, Daddy?"

And like a bucket of cold water was thrown over Vidar, he jerked out of his spell and looked away. He hated that word. He wasn't a daddy and didn't kink shame. He probably would have loved to be a Daddy to some sweet boy but hearing the word from Boyd brought far too many unpleasant memories. Like a movie trailer, he remembered the snippets of hearing Boyd call Sasha that as he grunted and moaned and cried out his release. No, he hated the term Daddy, and it was enough of a distraction and gut-wrenching ache that his blood pressure lowered and with it, his erection. He didn't look at Boyd, but he saw the little divot between his brows. Of course he was confused. Vidar went from *rip my clothes off* to *get me the hell out of here* in two seconds.

"I... I need to go." Vidar stood slowly to not hurt Boyd who still knelt between his legs. Boyd sat back on his heels.

"What?" Boyd questioned. Vidar stood and hurried to the door. "Vidar, wait," Boyd called after him.

He stopped, one hand on the door handle and the other clenched into a fist at his side. "I'm sorry. It's not you." He then heaved a sigh and turned seeing Boyd had followed him to the entryway. "You are beautiful and were stunning on that pole but... I can't. I'm sorry. It's not you, it's me." As soon as he said it, Boyd crossed his arms over his chest and looked away.

"Yeah, sure, whatever," he turned his back to Vidar. Wanting to go to him, and wanting desperately to leave, Vidar was torn. But as soon as Boyd left his sight, going back into the living room, Vidar remembered the sounds, the pain of hearing Boyd cry out in ecstasy, the betrayal he felt when Boyd had dismissed him in favor of Sasha. Sasha, the Russian agent turned traitor.

With a deep breath, a mumbled "sorry", Vidar opened the door and made his escape.

Chapter Seven

What the hell? Boyd paced in his dim living room, the pole still revealed and the lights low. He had danced his heart out on that pole with the help of Queen Miley and Vidar *left?!* He was into it, Boyd was certain. He felt the evidence himself. So why? What had changed? What turned him cold as a fish out of water?

As he paced, huffing at the indignation, his mind raced attempting to figure out what was going on. After far too long, in his opinion, he let out a feral growl and moved his hands in a downward motion.

"Enough," he took a breath and made a decision. Pushing the button on the wall, he watched the plaster and drywall encase the dance pole. "LOVE," he called to his AI assistant. "Raise lights to seventy-five percent and the curtains all the way."

"Sure, Baby." The voice replied and he grinned. He had created the AI LOVE: Language and Order Virtual Engineer a few years ago and updated her voice.

Once the lights were up, he turned on his Miley playlist and began to dance like a music video, as if no one watched and he loved the freedom. After the song ended the second time, he let it go to the next one and headed to the primary bathroom.

Running a shower, he entered under the spray and let out a long moan. It was heavenly to be in his own bathroom. He decidedly did not think of Vidar. He refused. But why did he turn so cold so quickly? *Ugh, no.*

He would get no answers. And he refused to let the joy of being home be wrecked by the one man he wanted to share his space with. Not one of the CCB knew he danced; they had only seen him do yoga in the office. He hadn't told anyone and the one time he let someone in… well, never again. Two could play whatever game Vidar was playing and Boyd was excellent at games.

Boyd reveled in the shower and once dried, he pulled on a pair of tight leggings sans pants and a crop top sweatshirt from one of the local shops. Whipping up a light dinner of boiled chicken, veggies, and rice he sat on the sofa and flicked through the channels on the tele. Nothing caught his eye but before he landed on BBC News. An anchor spoke, and Boyd listened curiously.

"Parliament is expected to vote today on the historic Prison Reform Bill gaining bi-partisan support from both Tories and Labour parties. The bill will allow a much-needed look into sentencing and will also offer a small measure of hope to those currently incarcerated. This coming on the heels of several strikes happening throughout Great Britain in the Prison Guard Unions. Leaders of both parties claim that, if passed, this bill will be revolutionary and will conquer the issues currently facing British prisons including overcrowding and under budgeting. Other circumstances surrounding the bill will be discussed. But it is thought that once passed, some lucky families will be reunited with loved ones as early as next week. We go now to our BBC correspondent for more on this."

Boyd changed the channel and shook his head. Yes, reform needed to happen. But he was concerned about who they would let out and how reintegration would affect the city.

Dinner done, he watched another episode of Drag Race and took notes on the makeup application from one of his favorite drag queens. The sun was starting its descent in the sky and a glance at the clock told him it would be dusk soon. Taking his keys, he turned off the tele and locked up his apartment. His nightly walk was a time he always enjoyed. The peace. The alone time. The harmony with nature, all the wonderful sights and smells. He lived in a diverse area and always enjoyed seeing the different cultures and smelling the amazing foods. But his usual thirty-minute walk ended up being an hour and a half. He needed the time away to think but he came to no conclusions. He barely remembered walking through town and only when he came upon a red brick building in the historic portion of Westminster, did he know where he was. Vidar's flat.

He stared at it for a long moment. The spattering of lights poured out of some windows, while the muted glow of others showed curtains were drawn. The sun's remaining rays weren't enough to light the sky and streetlamps clicked on, basking Boyd in artificial light. His thinking had led him there.

Selfishly, he wanted to know why Vidar left and why he still fought their connection. He knew he was being a hypocrite. He had deliberately fought their smolder for months. Taking Sasha to bed, he was deliberately loud knowing Vidar was in the other room. He wanted him to man up. Boyd didn't play with straight guys. And for all intents and purposes, Vidar was a straight guy. He had yet to tell Boyd how he identified but Boyd knew he hadn't been with a man. But when he held him... Boyd sighed. He never felt safer than when he had Vidar's thick arms around him. His cologne teased his nose every day, that fresh water, cooling mountain air mixed with subtle wood and spices that tickled his nose and made him want to gulp in breath after breath.

He was tired of not allowing himself to be with him, hence the pole dance. It was an invitation and Vidar had refused. Boyd needed to know why. Never considering himself an insecure person, he hated the feeling of... inadequacy. Shaking his head, he stepped up to the front door.

Also, he thought harshly. *Who the hell was Vidar speaking to on the phone?*

The man may not be his, but Boyd was jealous and possessive of what he considered *his.* And Vidar was his. He buzzed Vidar's flat.

"Yes?" He heard Vidar's voice, hollow from the intercom.

"It's me, let me in," Boyd said.

There was silence for a long moment, then, "where is the dead center of London?"

Seriously? Boyd questioned. The start of the riddle, though the answer was well known, was code in their team. The answer depended on the situation. If the agent was in distress, the answer was "I am." If the agent needed evac due to being followed or cover blown the answer was "The Thames." But if all was well, and they simply needed to identify one another, they each had a special response based on their codename.

"Mount Parnassus," Boyd answered. Again, Vidar seemed to hesitate, but eventually Boyd heard the buzz at the door indicating he had been let in. Once inside, he marched down the hallway to the main stairs. Vidar's flat was on the third floor of the five-story building. Every agent in CCB knew where everyone lived, and they were tested on it regularly.

He reached Vidar's door, and it was his turn to hesitate. But he shook himself out of it and cleared his throat. Raising his fist to knock, he ignored the sweat trickling down his back. Knocking sharply, he instantly backed away from the door when a menacing bark came from the other side.

"Sheila," Vidar's voice scolded before he opened the door. Boyd took in the image before him.

Vidar stood in dark joggers and an olive-green faded unit shirt. He was barefoot and holding the collar of a gigantic beast. Well... a German Shepard dog but the animal had to be seventy pounds. Boyd swallowed seeing its sharp teeth. He didn't like dogs or cats... or really any animal. He'd been bitten by a bulldog when he was five and the scars of trauma never healed.

"Boyd? Are you all right?" Vidar asked and Boyd shook himself out of his fear.

"I... came to talk," Boyd said.

Vidar stared at him for the longest time and Boyd would have given nearly anything to know what was going on inside Vidar's head. After a beat, Vidar nodded crisply once and pulled the dog back. The animal... *Sheila?*... didn't seem to want to go anywhere.

"Come on, Baby," Vidar coaxed, and Boyd's eyes grew wide. *Baby... he'd been talking to his dog?* "Sorry, she likes visitors too much, especially when I've been away. She's curious about you."

Boyd didn't know what sound had escaped him, but he was sure he sounded like a child with a mix of hysterical thrown in.

"Do you... are you afraid of dogs?" Vidar asked cautiously watching him.

"Dogs... cats... horses... pretty much anything that can bite me."

"Sheila won't bite. Will you, girl? Promise." Vidar offered his hand to Boyd and almost like he was in a trance, Boyd took Vidar's hand, swallowing hard and letting him curl his fingers into a loose fist. "Let her smell you."

Vidar crouched down next to his dog, petting her, holding her back gently but firmly. Boyd lowered his fist putting all his fear away as best he could. He wasn't sure how he trusted this beast, but one look in her dark brown eyes and Boyd smiled slightly. Sheila cautiously leaned forward and sniffed Boyd's hand. After a moment, her tongue slipped out and licked his knuckles. Boyd giggled and flattened his hand on her silky head petting her.

"Scratch here and she'll love you forever," Vidar spoke softly showing Boyd where, behind her ear, Sheila liked to be scratched. "That's it. You're really a big softie aren't you, baby?"

Boyd looked over at Vidar, suddenly surprised to see how close they were to each other. Mere inches separated their lips when they looked at each other. Sheila snuffled around them both,

A short whistle echoed across the room and the spell

between them broke as Sheila let out a playful bark and bounded further into the living room. Boyd stood quickly, eyeing the room. Only then did he realize they were not alone. Two men sat opposite each other in two wingback chairs in the living room. One was lavishing attention on Sheila while the other took in the scene before him. His sharp gaze more pronounced by his tanned skin and high cheekbones. He was of Asian descent, Boyd saw, but he wasn't sure which country. He was handsome in an exotic way and had a strong bearing, even sitting across the room, that Boyd averted his eyes. The other man was pale with dark brown hair, light eyes, and a bit of a five o'clock shadow covering his face and neck. They were both looking at him curiously, whiskey glasses in their hands and their ankles crossed over their knees.

"Oh," Boyd breathed. "I didn't realize you had company."

"It's okay," Vidar said.

"I should… go," Boyd turned.

"No, you don't have to," Vidar hurried and grabbed his upper arm gently. Boyd looked up into Vidar's deep blue eyes and wished for the thousandth time that he could read him or that Vidar would talk to him and tell him what he truly thought.

"He might be inclined to stay if you introduce us, Vi," the paler one said. His accent showed he grew up in Wales.

"Right," Vidar looked at him and shrugged. Boyd let out a soft chuckle and nodded. Vidar gave him a grin and walked over to his friends.

The Asian man stood as they approached, and Boyd cowered at the intensity of his stare and in the shadow of his six-foot two-inch frame.

"Boyd, this is Gareth Godwin and his husband Dae-Hyun Lee. Lads, this is Boyd Falstaff."

"Good to meet you," Gareth said offering his hand to Boyd as he stood too. Boyd had always been on the shorter side, he barely reached 5'8" and he was fine with it but staring up at Godwin who stood two inches taller than his husband and shorter than Vidar, Boyd took a step back. He was surrounded by three very tall men and his breathing became erratic. He hated being in that situation. He was stronger than when he was a boy, and the circumstances were different, but the situation was far too similar. They could overpower him. Hurt him. Just like his rapists did. He couldn't catch his breath. They were talking around him, and Dae-Hyun took a step toward him, but Boyd didn't hear anything they were saying. He had to get out of there. Cursing himself for the weakness, he hadn't had a random PTSD attack in years. But then he felt something warm and wet on his hand. Looking down suddenly, Sheila was there staring up at him and just nudging his hand with her snout. She licked his fingers, and her whine broke through his haze. Boyd took a deep breath and crouched down to be level with his new best friend. Sheila licked his chin and cheeks, nuzzling his neck and huffing into his shoulder.

"Thank you, baby girl," he whispered. The dog had sensed his panic attack and helped him. He didn't want to look up at the three men. He was pretty sure he had just made a horrible first impression. "Can you help me salvage my image to your daddy's friends?" He asked the dog. His answer was an additional lick and her walking to his side, sitting next to him, facing the three men, her tail hitting his legs as it wagged. With a heaved sigh, he looked up to find both Vidar and Gareth sitting while Dae-Hyun stood a little in front of him, his hands out in a calming gesture.

"Breathe," Dae-Hyun said softly.

Boyd nodded and looked over at Vidar. His face was

compressed into a look of concern.

"Sorry about that." He tried to sound like his normal self but failed. "I don't do well being surrounded by strangers... tall strangers. What a bloody terrible first impression. Sorry."

"Don't be," Dae-Hyun said kindly.

"You're with three old soldiers, mate," Gareth replied. "We know PTSD when we see it. Don't apologize for something beyond your control."

"Well that... makes me feel better," he admitted.

"Sit? Drink?" Vidar offered.

Gareth chuckled. "You're worse than Dae, Vi," he said. "Are you capable of saying more than two words?"

"At least I can create full sentences," Dae-Hyun teased.

"Sorry," Vidar looked away then back at Boyd. "Would you like to sit down? Can I get you something to drink?"

"It's a miracle," Boyd gasped teasingly. "I might have to keep you two around."

Laughter at Vidar's expense echoed, and Boyd hoped he didn't mind. With an indulgent smirk on his handsome face, Vidar stood. "Beer? Whiskey?"

"Is the kid old enough to drink, Vi?" Gareth asked with a wink.

"And old enough for more fun pursuits," Boyd answered with a lick on his upper lip.

Gareth chuckled and his husband shook his head but had a relaxed grin on his face as he sat in the chair opposite Gareth. "I'll do a beer, thank you," Boyd answered and took the spot on the sofa opposite where Vidar had been sitting. "So, how do you all know each other?" Boyd asked as Vidar headed to the kitchen to get Boyd's beer.

Chapter Eight

Vidar tuned out the conversation as he headed to the kitchen. Having returned home after Boyd's incredible dance and blatant invitation to sleep with him, he had hurried into the shower after texting Godwin and Lee. They had been looking after Sheila for him and his Baby Girl was so happy to see him. She had pounced and knocked him back in the entryway, then proceeded to lick his face, jump around him, and wag her whole body. He reveled in her love.

After pouring them both a glass of whiskey, they sat down, and Gareth looked at Dae-Hyun, then spoke. "What's going on, Vi?"

Vidar had sighed, wiped a hand down his face, took a swig of beer and launched into his predicament. "There's this... guy."

He told his best friends about Boyd and his reaction to him and waited for their advice. After a few minutes, his front door buzzer sounded. He nearly died when he heard Boyd's voice on the intercom. The hesitation and asking their code were so he could have time to plead his friends for help. They were of little assistance. Godwin just grinned and gave him a little hip thrust and Dae rolled his eyes (at his husband or at Vidar, he wasn't sure) and told him to buzz Boyd in.

Now, Boyd sat in Vidar's living room waiting for a beer with Sheila at his side. Vidar had never been so scared as earlier when Boyd went completely pale. His full beautifully pink lips had lost all color and Sheila had started to whine. A panic attack. Sheila was not only their bomb sniffing dog, but she was also trained in recognizing the symptoms of PTSD and panic attacks in soldiers. Dae had told both he and Gareth to sit and tried to speak calmly to Boyd. It had taken everything inside him not to take Boyd into his arms and chase away the demons in his past. But it proved to Vidar just how little he knew about Boyd. They had never had a proper talk. One where they got to know each other.

The man joked a lot... too much, and Vidar couldn't decipher fact from fiction. He didn't know him, but he wanted to. He wanted to know everything about him. He knew they needed to learn to trust each other and maybe he could put himself out there. Maybe he could finally admit to him he was gay, and he wanted Boyd. He ached for him. But he might never feel comfortable, and he didn't know how to break that hold over him. He flinched when Godwin slapped his hand on his thigh, with a boisterous laugh. The sudden sound of a heavy hand striking reminded him too much of other things. His father's screaming voice echoed in his head. Shaking the image away, he refused to give it power. Easier said than done but there had already been one panic attack amongst them, he didn't want another. With a deep breath, he headed back to the living room hearing his best friends laughing with Boyd.

"He got an eyeful, that's for damn sure," Godwin was saying between wheezes for breath.

"Mortifying," Lee agreed.

"Oh, baby, you liked the idea of almost getting caught." Godwin winked.

"Almost," Dae stressed. "There's a kink for *almost.* But not getting caught with my cock in your ass in the showers."

Vidar laughed. He remembered the story they were sharing. He had caught them at it in the barracks' showers and after the initial shock had said something and walked away.

"We heard you hooking up every night in the bunks, what makes seeing it any different?" Vidar questioned as he handed Boyd his beer. Their fingers touched and Boyd smiled up at him. The lightness in his eyes was breathtaking.

"The difference was being seen and you offering to make up a third," Lee answered.

Boyd nearly choked on his beer and Vidar closed his eyes. So *that* was what he had said. He'd been so embarrassed and turned on at the same time, he thought he'd made some quip about them getting off, but he didn't remember.

"You what?" Boyd coughed while laughing. "You sure it was this guy?"

"Quite sure," Lee answered. "And get him comfortable with you, he actually speaks more than in grunts and monosyllables. Get on his friend side and he might make jokes."

"Gasp!" Boyd teased. "Say it ain't so!"

"I honestly don't remember what I said. I was dying from secondhand embarrassment," Vidar replied.

"No, you were dying from your own embarrassment. There was none of us," Godwin winked. "Oh and you said, and I quote," he leaned forward and cleared his throat. "'Seems like you lads got it handled. Want to handle mine too?' To which Dae replied, 'we're game if you are' and you ran away. Left us. Interrupted us and left us. So rude."

Vidar gave him the two-finger salute and took a desperate sip of his beer and washed away the image of his two best friends naked and hard.

"So, Vi tells us you two work together," Dae-Hyun said, changing the subject.

Boyd nodded and took a drink, looking sideways at Vidar.

"They know some of what we do," Vidar explained.

"Only that you work for a top-secret team and all of you are on the rainbow spectrum?" Godwin teased. "So jealous."

"Don't be," Boyd answered. "No fraternization policy."

"Otherwise you'd jump our boy's bones?" Dae asked.

"Dae..." Vidar shook his head.

"Yeah, exactly that," Boyd surprised him.

"Would anyone know?" Dae asked.

"Pretty sure everyone would," Boyd replied. "Though it didn't stop our boss from marrying one of our teammates and two others getting engaged."

"So... what's stopping you?" Godwin asked leaning forward and setting his drink down on the coffee table and petting Sheila as she walked past him to sit on her doggy bed.

"I'm a rule follower." Boyd's faux innocent look didn't stop Godwin.

Barking a laugh, Godwin spoke, "Right, and I'm straighter than an arrow."

"News to me, babe," Dae winked at his husband.

"Don't put him on the spot, lads. Maybe he doesn't like me," Vidar said.

"Impossible, what's not to like?" Dae asked.

"Well, I only recently came out myself. My dad's an arse when it comes to gay people, and I'm petrified he'll find out because when I tried on my mum's makeup at five, he beat the shite out of me. When I told him I wanted to take dance lessons, he nearly broke my leg with the car door. So I have issues he doesn't need." Vidar didn't realize he was panting until it became loud in the silence that followed. He looked at his two best friends, but Godwin and Lee looked down and took a breath. They knew he had a rough childhood. His dad's anger issues were well documented in the press; the joy of being a professional athlete's family.

His eyes scanned the room coming to rest on Boyd who was staring at him, no judgement, just concern. Boyd said nothing as he crawled over the couch and pulled Vidar's arms open and piled into his lap. Vidar was still and stiff as a marble statue. But Boyd wasn't deterred. He nuzzled his face into Vidar's neck and held him. After a moment, Vidar closed his eyes and wrapped his arms around Boyd, holding him tightly.

"I'm so sorry you went through that," he whispered against Vidar's neck.

Not knowing how to reply, Vidar tightened his hold on Boyd and closed his eyes. It wasn't until he heard movement that he opened his eyes. Gareth and Dae-Hyun were gathering their things. He caught Gareth's eye.

"We'll head out," he winked. "Want us to take Sheila or want to drop her off in the morning?"

"Drop her off," he answered. "Thanks, Gare, Dae."

"Take care," Dae said squeezing Vidar's shoulder as he passed and smiled down at Boyd. "Good to meet you, Boyd. See you again soon."

Boyd nodded and replied with *goodbye* and *see you again soon*. The door closed softly behind his best friends and Vidar heard them lock the door using their key, but he didn't move.

"Do you want to talk about it?" Boyd finally asked.

Vidar closed his eyes for a moment but as soon as he opened them again and looked down at Boyd, still in his lap and wrapped in his arms, he knew it was time to open up to him if he ever wanted to see where the relationship could go. He nodded and when Boyd moved as if to slip off his lap, he tightened his arms around him. Boyd searched his face for something, and Vidar tried to keep his expression open. Whatever Boyd was looking for, he must have found it because he settled against Vidar's chest and rested his head on Vidar's shoulder. It felt right. It felt good and Vidar never wanted to let go.

"My father had anger issues. It's well documented in the *Daily Mail* and all other forms of press. He'd been red carded from several games for causing fights on the pitch. He even got benched for five games for deliberately injuring a teammate. But he was good, so the coach told him to shape up or he was off the team. So he did. Without the constant release of anger against grown men, he turned it on my mum and me. She left him, but since she had dropped out of Uni when she'd gotten pregnant with me at eighteen, it was decided I would leave my grandparents in Norway and live in England with my dad full time. My mum's parents died

72

when I was really young, and she turned to my dad's parents. They were amazing. Still are. They're in their nineties now but I still try to go see them whenever I can. I stayed with them during the off season when dad had less time at games and more time training.

"But when I was twelve, I moved to England to live with my dad alone. He left me mainly on my own as he only had a few years left playing professionally. When he wasn't playing, he had no outlet for his anger. He had caught me at five playing with my mum's makeup and beat me. Ever since then, he gave me a weekly beating whether I deserved it or not. And I'm not talking about spanking, he used his fists and belts. I guess, he always said he was trying to make me a man.

"His teammates used to step in and try to protect me. I remember my dad left me at the training facility to go to the pub and the captain took me home to stay with his wife and kids. He was so nice. I felt like a fish out of water seeing how kind he was to his family and how sweet they were to me. But my dad came to collect me the next morning and Cap could do nothing to stop him. I still remember the look on his face when I turned to thank him. There were tears in his eyes."

"Do you still talk to him?"

"Yeah, he's the manager now. I followed his career, and we reconnected when I got out of the Army."

"He's more like a dad to you, huh?"

Vidar smiled slightly and nodded. "I remember a time dad got so angry on the pitch when no one was passing him the ball even when he was wide open. A few players even knocked him down a few times. Cap told me some of the boys had seen what he'd done to me and were trying to teach him a lesson. Trash-talking him calling him names. Saying he's a pussy for hitting a child. Dad lost it. He was benched for three games."

"They looked out for you."

"On the pitch, yeah. But when it was just us..." Vidar shuddered. "I remember when I told my dad I wanted to take up dance. As I said earlier, he nearly broke my leg slamming the car door on it repeatedly. I was lying in the hospital bed when a Social Worker came in to talk to me. She told me I had options, but I was scared. I knew no one in England and barely understood the language. I lied and told her I fell. She didn't push me but left me her card. Dad saw it and for once seemed genuinely sorry for what he had done. He got some help. Weekly meetings with the team's psychologist. But ManU lost the year after he retired, and he took up drinking. I remember that night. I was fifteen and he came stumbling home screaming my name." Vidar took a moment to collect himself. "When the war in the Middle East began, I was fourteen. I joined the school's premilitary organization and learned how to defend myself. Then, joined up when I could. I never looked back. I still talk to my dad. He's trying. I think he's scared of me now. He's not as big as me. I don't know. If he finds out I'm... whatever I am, he..." Vidar breathed.

Boyd was quiet for a long moment but soon, Vidar felt the soft fluttering kisses on his neck and Boyd snuggled deeper into his chest.

"I'm sorry that happened to you," Boyd said softly, and Vidar felt the words to the marrow of his bones. "No one should ever treat another person that way, let alone a child. But you got away. You are whole. Yes, you're missing a part of you inside, the spot a father's love is supposed to fill but that just means someone else can fill their spot inside your heart to overflowing and maybe the little holes can be filled with another kind of love."

Vidar stared at him taking in his beautiful face, so open and loving. Cupping his cheek, they locked eyes. "Some call you a nymph, others a siren, but one thing I know is, from the first moment I saw you, you had me mind, body, and soul. If I didn't know any better, I'd worry you were a witch. I've never been under a spell before but I'm pretty sure this is what it feels like."

"I'm not a witch," Boyd breathed. "And I've been yours since that first moment I saw you walk in with Kiter. I was just scared, still am."

"Me too."

"I want you more than I've ever wanted anyone but it's more than that. I want to wake up with you, cuddle with you and Sheila on the couch. I want to take her for walks and stop off at our favorite coffee shop. I want breakfast in bed with slow kisses and gentle touches. I want to make love to you. I've never had any of that. I don't know if I'll ever get my happily ever after because I don't know if that's something you want too. I pushed you away because I've had so much disappointment and hurt in my life. I don't think I could handle you rejecting me. I've only ever filled my life with meaningless, nameless hookups, I've never had a real relationship. Everyone I love dies or leaves me alone and I get through it. But if you left me, I don't think I could. It would destroy me. I didn't put a spell on you Vidar Jørgensen, but I sure as hell, am under yours and I don't ever want to lose you."

Vidar leaned his forehead against Boyd's. "I'm scared too. I've never done this with a guy and all my previous girlfriends... which there have only been three serious ones, have told me they felt secondary to my career. They never thought I was very good in bed, either. But see, I never felt the way I knew I was supposed to feel for them. All my mates in my platoon talked about their women and how much they loved sex and how amazing it was... I just never felt that. Until now. I want it to crawl under your skin to be one with you and never let you go. I want to hold you forever and be the reason you smile. I want to catch your eye across the room and know what you're thinking. Share a little smile only we understand. I want to go out with you and sneak out of parties just to come home and be together with Sheila by our side. I want to take care of you. I want to bring you coffee in bed. I want to cook for you. I want to come home to you and see you playing with Sheila. I want to support you in everything you want to do. And I really want to watch you dance again... that was... wow."

Boyd grinned and Vidar wiped his stray tear from his cheek.

"I know I come with a lot of baggage and trauma. I know that I know nothing about gay sex and a relationship between two men. And I know you'll have to teach me a lot, but I want to risk it because I know in my heart we're meant for each other."

Boyd hesitated and Vidar's heart nearly stopped, but he waited and let him process. It was a solid twenty-five seconds before Boyd spoke.

"I was gang raped for child pornography when I was eleven and nearly every night after that at the orphanage. We were kids, the oldest was my bunkmate Jack. He protected us as best he could, but they wanted fresh blood. The more we screamed, the more money they made. It was a Catholic orphanage for nearly a year before the state took it over. That's when he arrived. The Warden, Jacob McMasters. He was the first. He filmed it and sold it on the dark web. Two years after the first time it happened, Jack tried to stand up against them. He was beaten and we suffered for it. Another time, he tried to run to the police who were in the area investigating some convenience store robbery. But the warden caught him, and they beat him up in front of us. He didn't scream. He knew they wanted him to. But he defiantly looked at the warden as the men punched him and didn't scream. He was tossed back in our bunk, and I tried to help him, but I was dragged away. He tried to stop them, but he couldn't move. When I was tossed back into the room after their... filming, Jack wasn't in bed. I asked around but no one knew what happened to him. At least, no one was willing to say. I still don't know where he is or what happened. He's probably dead and buried on the land somewhere but I would like to know."

"Then we'll find out. We'll look for him. Use MI6's database and with the team's help, we'll find him. Maybe he's alive, maybe not. But you'll know. After this case, you'll know," Vidar promised holding him tighter. The emotions swirling in his head threatened to consume him. He could see Little Boyd in his mind's eye and all he wanted was to hold that scared eleven-year-old and tell him what an amazing man he grew up to be. Instead, he held Adult Boyd on his lap and rocked him.

"I got them. I got all of them," his voice was so quiet, Vidar wasn't sure he had heard correctly.

"What do you mean?" Vidar made his tone soft and let it resonate deep in his chest. Boyd snuggled deeper, almost like a cat.

"I got out of there at fifteen. When I was sixteen, I grifted the warden. Made him think I was into it, and he took me back to his place. I didn't let him do anything to me. I'd drugged his last drink at the pub and searched his place for the pictures and videos. When he passed out, I found everything. Money that changed hands, videos, pictures, everything. Before he woke, I called the police and told them where the porn stash was. The cops found it and arrested him. They couldn't try him for the rapes because of the limitations set by the law, but he got fifteen years for possession of child pornography. He still has about ten years left. Then, I found every single one of the men who worked there. Every one of the ones who had raped me. I found them all and sent them to jail one after the other. I was there for every one of their sentencings. They all saw me in the visitors' section. My grinning face was the last thing they saw before they were taken back to their cells. Some of them screamed at me. Others cried. It was… cathartic and a little evil."

"The evil was done to you. It was not evil to get revenge and you did so through the legal way."

"I got them all." Boyd continued as if he hadn't heard Vidar. Vi stroked his back softly letting him talk. "I realized I was good at it. I was on the streets and heard things. When I got full stories, I went after others too. I taught myself everything I could to hack the dark web and get the videos of me and the other boys down. I traced IP addresses of everyone who had seen or purchased the videos and collected the research. I sent it all to MI5 under the name Autolycus. They took action and the men were all arrested but more keep popping up. It's a never-ending cycle of torture, trauma, and pain and I'm tired of it."

"You are so brave. So strong to have gone through all of that alone. It was the most painful thing, but it made you stronger. But baby," Vidar nudged him to look up at him. "You don't have to be strong with me."

In that moment, Boyd clutched him tighter and burst into tears. Vidar let him cry, soothing him, as he let out years of pain. Vidar wanted to kill McMasters for the horrific pain he caused.

When Boyd finally calmed down enough to breathe, he still didn't move, and Vidar was in no hurry for him to go anywhere.

"Thank you," he hiccupped.

"For what?" Vidar asked.

"Letting me cry it out. It's been a tough day and it's the anniversary of my grandfather's death. I really needed an outlet, hence the dancing."

"And the attempted seduction?" Vidar grinned.

"Guilty," Boyd chuckled and pulled back to look up into Vidar's eyes. "I'd still like to seduce you."

"And I'll let you, but not tonight."

"Why?"

"Because we've both processed some serious trauma and I don't want to have that in my head when I finally push inside you."

A blush-colored Boyd's cheeks and he looked away, then grinned and turned back. "Can I kiss you?"

Vidar's skin prickled with sudden desire, and he found himself nodding. He swallowed hard and licked his lips. Boyd moved slowly, tightening his arms around Vidar's neck and pressing their chests together. Keeping his eyes focused on Vidar, Boyd leaned a little further in. After a beat, Vidar realized what Boyd was waiting for. A soft smile lifted his lips, and he leaned the rest of the way. Pressing his lips to Boyd's, he let out a soft moan. He was home.

Chapter Nine

Vidar tasted of whiskey and man and Boyd loved every sip. His lips were smooth and warm, hesitant, but sweet. Boyd didn't push but he ran his tongue across the seam of Vidar's lips and on his gasp took the opportunity to plunge his tongue into his mouth. The flavor of *man* increased, and Boyd moaned pulling himself tighter against him.

When Vidar's tongue tentatively caressed his, Boyd gasped. All the blood in his body pooling at his groin made him lightheaded.

Growing bolder, Vidar sucked on Boyd's tongue causing him to whimper and tighten his hold. The feel of his calloused big hands lifting the back of his t-shirt and stroking the soft skin of his lower back excited him even more. He moved his lower body to straddle Vidar's hips feeling his very prominent erection behind his loose joggers. As Vidar sipped at his lips, Boyd rubbed against him trying and failing for the friction his lower body so desperately needed.

Vidar grunted as Boyd's clothed erection rubbed against his and Boyd pushed himself up again. Landing with a bounce on Vidar's lap, the man in his arms grunted and broke their kiss, panting.

"What are you doing to me?" He breathed, resting his forehead against Boyd's.

"Just showing you how much I want you," Boyd replied using his nails to scratch softly at the back of Vidar's head.

"You're killing me."

"The French call it *le petite mort* for a reason." His breathing was still labored. Vidar pulled back fully and stared at him for a long time before Boyd grinned. "So, how was your second first kiss with a guy?"

Vidar smiled. "In some ways, better than the first, first kiss with a guy."

"Some ways?" Boyd pouted.

"First kisses are special, you know?" Vidar's tone was teasing but Boyd huffed and crossed his arms over his chest.

"Rude." Grinning, Vidar's face lit up and the beauty stopped Boyd in his thoughts. "You are so beautiful."

Vi's smile slowly softened, and he cupped Boyd's face. "If I am, then I don't have the corner market on that. You bewitched me from the moment I saw you and I've never wanted anyone more."

Boyd nuzzled into his hand and sighed. "Can I stay? I don't

want to walk back."

"Walk? You walked here? It's over ten kilometers."

Boyd nodded. "I usually take a walk at night but this time I needed to see you. Sorry for interrupting your time with your friends."

"Don't be. They called me earlier to video chat with Sheila and I was able to get home to see her for the evening." Sheila looked up at them both from her bed in the corner, her tail beginning to wag. "They were dog sitting for me."

"Your friends seem like fun."

"They are. And their story is so interesting. They were both completely straight when they entered the military. Partnered as sniper and scope they were together twenty-four-seven. It was a natural progression I guess. The first time we all heard them hooking up, we glanced at each other. Our commander, he's also bi and never hid his sexuality from us, just shrugged and rolled over. I was up the entire time wondering why I had a raging hard on."

"Was that the first time you were ever exposed to gay sex?"

"I'd stumbled on MMF porn and found it pretty hot, but I always felt guilty. Like my dad's voice in my head telling me I was a freak, unnatural, I got out of it before I could see anything. That little story they told you about me catching them? That was the day right after the first time we heard them, and I'd never wanked so much. I was so unbelievably turned on and yet scared shitless."

Boyd giggled. "I would have paid money to have seen your face."

"Redder than a tomato, I'm sure."

They were quiet for a long moment content to hold each

other until Vidar sighed a happy sigh and leaned back. "Are you hungry?" He asked.

Boyd shook his head. "I ate before I left and it's a little too late now."

Glancing at the clock behind him, Vidar paused. "I didn't realize it was so late. Tired?"

"Yeah." Boyd's voice was muffled by Vidar's shirt, and he felt himself falling asleep in Vidar's arms.

"Come on," he whispered and gathered Boyd firmly against his chest before he stood. Boyd held on to Vidar's neck and wrapped his legs around his waist. "I won't drop you."

"I know." And he did, he trusted Vidar implicitly.

"Stay, baby girl," he called to Sheila as her tail began wagging.

"Does she usually sleep with you?" Boyd asked locking eyes with the dog.

"Sometimes, but never when I have someone over," Vidar explained. "I think she just missed me."

"If you want her to, I don't mind."

"I should take you to the guest room," Vidar chuckled. "I shouldn't want to keep you all to myself. I should do a lot of things. But right now, I just want you in my arms. Do you mind?"

"Oh, so difficult," Boyd teased. "I have to spend the night with a hot guy wrapped all up in his strong arms, cozy and safe. I mean that's just horrible. Poor me."

Vidar's chuckle resounded in his chest as he set Boyd on his feet. The soft plush carpet squishing between his toes. Boyd didn't release him as he wrapped his arms around his neck.

"Thank you," he said softly.

Vidar squeezed him tightly for a moment. "I feel like I

should be saying thank you to you."

"Don't thank me yet." Boyd's voice held a playful tone. "I usually sleep nude."

Vidar's arms tightened once more, and his lips glanced off his ear. "So do I."

Boyd bit his lip as a moan threatened to escape. The thought of Vidar's naked body pressed against his, of being encapsulated in his strong arms as his massive chest and legs enveloped him, teased him with images causing certain body parts to react with gusto.

"No fair," he breathed.

Vidar chuckled, took one more deep inhale, and let him go. "Come on, if you need, bathroom's through there. You can use my toothbrush if you want."

Boyd agreed and hurriedly went to the bathroom. Once he was done, he opened the medicine cabinet on the wall and snooped. Vidar had the usual things, eye drops, plasters, tweezers, shaver heads. But he also noticed an open box of condoms... not just any but XL Magnums.

"Our boy is packing," he whispered again to himself as he grabbed one of the foil packets and slipped it into the one pocket of his leggings. The next thing he saw was a large box of cologne, one fairly popular in the early 2000s but Boyd couldn't remember the smell. Opening the black box with silver lettering and a raindrop holding the Norwegian flag, he took out the bottle and pulled off the silver top with a pop. Finding the sprayer, he put it under his nose and breathed in, groaning. The smell was the one he loved whenever Vidar walked past. It was clean, crisp with a hint of herbs and wood. Vidar's signature scent. And he loved it. Spraying a single spritz on his chest, Boyd closed it up and headed back to the bedroom. Vidar was pulling the sheets down on the bed and glanced up at him, sniffing.

"Did you spray my cologne?" He grinned.

"Not sorry," Boyd sang as he slipped out of his leggings and stood before Vidar, nude. "It smells like you, and I like it."

He watched Vidar swallow as he took in his naked body. "Like I said, I sleep nude. Didn't even have pants on."

Vidar gave a very tight nod and Boyd thought it was cute how turned on he was. The outline reminding Boyd of the condoms he found.

"Your turn," he said, and Vidar's eyes bounced from him to the bathroom door. With a quick excuse, he hurried to brush his teeth and Boyd listened to the soft running water and the *tap tap tap* of the toothbrush on the sink. Soon, his man reappeared in the doorway looking even better than before if that was possible. Boyd realized with a start, he had missed him in that short minute he'd been gone.

Not good. He was too far gone for him already.

Vidar stripped out of his shirt and joggers but didn't remove his underpants. The black tight briefs teased Boyd's senses and he pointedly looked up at him.

"If I don't leave something on, we won't just sleep," Vidar answered as if reading his mind.

"That's supposed to deter me?" Boyd teased, watching as Vidar moved to the other side of the bed and slipped between the sheets. He turned over to be able to watch him.

They lay there, Vidar not answering his rhetorical question. But one thing still bothered him. He moved closer and smiled as Vidar opened his arms to him. Laying his head on Vidar's chest, he spoke softly. "Why did you leave so quickly earlier? Did I say something wrong?"

Vidar paused, then took a deep breath. "You called me Daddy."

Boyd let his words seep in before he replied. "I'm sorry. I won't call you that if it bothers you."

"It's not that," Vidar interrupted. "I honestly would have found it unbelievably hot it not for…"

"Not for what?" Boyd prompted.

Heaving a sigh, Boyd felt the pain in Vidar's voice. "Sasha."

Boyd froze. "What… what about him?"

"You called Sasha Daddy that night. I could hear everything, and I guess you calling me that brought it all back. The pain, the bad memories."

Boyd closed his eyes and snuggled deeper into Vidar's side, kissing his chest softly. "I'm sorry. I… I'm an arse. I hated the idea that I wanted you and couldn't have you. I get mean. It's a defense mechanism. It's not right. I was also being a dick and being loud deliberately to make you as miserable as I was. I wanted it to be you. But I had a shitty way of showing it. If it helps at all, he means nothing to me. I was attracted to him, so I don't want you to blame it all on him. He didn't use me that way. I wanted it, even if I feel sick admitting it. But I'm just so sorry. I like to be taken care of by a Daddy. I always have. But I won't call you that. I promise."

"I… want you to but maybe," he hesitated. "Not yet."

Boyd nodded. "Whenever, if ever you want it, let me know."

Vidar turned and kissed his head. "When I tried to defend you and you chose him, it hurt. But not as much as hearing you giving yourself to him when I wanted you so badly. But the next day? When Kiter got angry with us, you gave me hope when you let me help you. I confess I was worried you'd go back to Sasha, that's why I went for a walk in the woods. But when I got back, I saw him on the sofa watching football and your door was closed. It gave me more hope. I knew it wasn't the right time, but I stood outside your door for a long time just wishing I was strong enough to knock."

"I felt you. I knew you were out there. I was hoping you'd knock too. But you didn't."

"I chickened out."

"It's okay. Today, I pressed my ear to the wall to try to hear your voice. You were on the phone and just that dull drone was comforting. That's how I found out about your baby girl." He laughed.

"What?" Vidar grinned.

"Earlier today, after lunch, I overheard you on the phone. I pressed my ear to the wall at the bunker and heard your voice talking about a baby. I left because I got a little jealous. But now I know you were talking about Shelia."

"I wondered why you left."

"I was doing some makeup tutorial and I heard you."

"Makeup?"

"Yeah, I," he looked down. "I play with makeup and drag and stuff for fun and relaxing. But I love it. You missed a very beautiful look by the way." When Vidar didn't respond, Boyd leveraged on his elbow and looked down at him. "Are you okay with me doing that?"

Taking a breath, a tear gathered in Vidar's eye. "Will you teach me?"

Boyd's heart broke for him. Instantly, he remembered his

story about playing with his mother's makeup and his father beating him and his eyes grew moist. Nodding quickly, Boyd leaned down and kissed him gently. "Happy to, baby."

With those soft words and the connection between them formed deeply in their bones, Boyd rested his head on his new favorite pillow, Vidar's chest, and closed his eyes. Just before sleep took him, he hoped his nightmares stayed away but somehow he knew, even his nightmares knew not to hurt him in Vidar's arms. His man would destroy them. Just as Boyd would destroy anyone who hurt him.

Chapter Ten

Sheila woke them both at 0700 by pouncing on the bed and licking both their faces. After a quick good morning kiss, a walk, and breakfast, Vidar drove the three of them to Gareth and Dae-Hyun's home. Gareth opened the door with a wide smile and Sheila barked before bounding up to him.

"Hey, baby girl," Gareth cooed when she flipped over, demanding belly rubs.

"Thanks for doing this, Gare," Vidar said walking over with the extra lead.

"Of course," he answered. "It works out great because Dae just left for work. He'll be gone all day, so I'll have someone to play with other than myself."

Vidar chuckled. "Thought you were both retired."

"We are but you know my husband, isn't satisfied unless he's doing something. I told him he could do me all he wants but he just gave me that look, you know the one."

"Oh yes, *that* look," Vidar grinned. "Well, thank him for me. I'll keep you updated. Hopefully, we'll be back to normal soon."

"Don't even worry about it. She's welcome anytime. You take care of yourselves," Gareth ordered.

"We will," Boyd promised.

"Maybe when all this craziness dies down, we can get dinner," Gareth offered.

"I'd like that," Vidar answered.

"I was talking to your boy, Vi," Gareth grinned. "But you're welcome too." He winked.

Boyd chuckled. "I won't be making up a third in a Dae-Gare sandwich. But dinner I can do."

"Expensive date," Gareth grumbled good-naturedly. "Better stop giving me ideas. My birthday is coming up."

"Mine too," winking Boyd threaded his hand thought Vidar's arm and blew a kiss to Gareth and Sheila before turning them both to the car.

"Don't even joke about it," Vidar grumbled.

Boyd beamed. "Why, Jørgensen, I do believe you're jealous."

Vidar growled and pulled Boyd nearly into his lap. "I'm serious, baby. You're mine."

Boyd shivered in his arms. Taking immense pleasure in that reaction, Vidar kissed him hard and pushed him back in his seat. "Seatbelt."

"Yes, Dad—" Boyd cut himself off and said nothing more

before reaching for the belt.

Once Vidar heard it click into place he patted Boyd's knee. "Good boy."

Boyd groaned.

They were in the lift at MI6 HQ heading down to the bunker when Vidar slipped his hand into Boyd's. He smiled up at him and Vidar's heart fluttered.

"Do you want them to know?" Boyd asked.

"I think they're going to," Vidar answered. "If they don't already."

Boyd nodded. "Besides you've seen me naked," he winked. "Though you haven't returned the favor. But... at least I know the size of condoms you buy so I doubt I'll be disappointed."

The color rose up Vidar's neck to his cheeks. "What?"

"I snooped in your bathroom. Might have taken one as a souvenir."

"You're terrible."

"You love it." Boyd froze after he said those words, but Vidar didn't miss a beat. He took him in his arms and kissed him softly.

"I do."

Boyd swallowed hard and the lift door dinged. Vidar looked out as the doors opened and his stomach lurched. He nearly pushed Boyd away from him and stepped back so fast but fortunately the man laughing had his back to the lift. His vision darkened to a single point, the man, turning around as he still tasted his boyfriend's lip balm.

"There he is!" The man exclaimed loudly as his face broke

into a wide smile. He threw his arms open and bent his torso as if dribbling a ball, as he raced to Vidar. He couldn't move as the man grabbed him around his waist and tried to lift him. Vidar flinched as his skin pinched in the man's grip. "There's my boy! Ugh, you keep getting taller and bigger. I remember when I could pick you up no problem."

"Far?" He asked saying the word for Father in Norwegian. "What... what are you doing here?"

"I'm in town for the PFA awards and thought I'd come see where you work. You know your old man was asked to present this year. I was nearby and thought I'd swing by. Never been to MI6 but they have some major security upstairs. This guy recognized me and got me through. Just meeting the team," he motioned to Kiter. "What's the matter with you?" His dad grinned and slapped him on the arm. "Aren't you pleased to see me?"

Vidar shook himself out of his stupor and forced a smile. "Of course! Of course," he said again, a little less crack-y. He locked eyes with Boyd whose gaze projected strength and gave him the breath he needed to walk his father over to the group gathered in the room. *"Far,"* he began. "This is my team. You met Kiter, our boss," he then indicated Rhys. "And his husband, Leo."

"Husband?" His father snapped.

Vidar closed his eyes knowing what was coming.

"Pleasure to meet you, Mr. Jørgensen," Rhys said.

"Vi didn't tell me his boss was a gay," he answered.

"Does it matter?" Kiter questioned. His question sounded innocent but the vitriol in his eyes was enough to melt anything.

"I don't want you contaminating my boy, that's all."

"Far," Vidar tried and took in the looks around the team. He pleaded with his friends.

Kiter grinned but the dark look didn't change in his eyes. He wrapped his arm around Rhys' waist pulling him into his side. "Not to worry, Oskar. Gayness isn't spreadable. We don't contaminate."

"Ehum," Vidar garnered his father's attention. "These are Agent Diamond and Reaper. My dad Oskar Jørgensen. Reaper is a big fan of yours."

"Are you?" His father's eyes left Kiter and lightened on Gabe Collins. Almost immediately, Vidar saw the media mask fall over his father's demeanor.

"ManU annual ticket holder," Gabe answered shaking his hand.

"Well, it's always wonderful to meet a fan."

"These are my boys," Gabe indicated his sons who stood with their grandfather.

"Splendid, you boys play footy?" Oskar asked.

"Yes sir," the eldest said.

"Good, what are your positions?"

"Wing," the boy replied. "And my brother is a Forward."

"Must be fast."

"Yes sir," the youngest boy answered.

"Good for you."

"Far," Vidar called. "This is our Team Lead Agent Fraxinus and our... Agent Autolycus."

Boyd gave a smooth smile and handshake.

"Good to meet you all," Oskar said.

"Why don't you show your dad around the training area?" Kiter offered.

"That'd be great. I gotta meet with the managers at 10 but I'm free for dinner. If you have the time, show me your favorite spot." Vidar knew it was *not* a request.

Vidar glanced a Boyd and then Kiter but forced a smile indicating the hallway. He was certain his father didn't want to go to his favorite spot as the chippy was far too informal, and the pub he always went to with the team had the distinct pleasure of being the most famous gay bar in town. His father had a reputation he liked to maintain: Best and most expensive... everything.

They weren't far enough away from the team before his father spoke up. "Not sure how I like you being around gays."

"Far—"

"Just promise me you won't be going to any Pride events. Not my son. I have a boy, not a girl. You use that for anything other than pussy, I'll cut it off, you hear me? Disgusting freaks."

"Far, that's ridiculous."

"Good," he nodded once. "I don't have a fag for a son."

"Oh hell no." Vidar heard Boyd's voice and he prayed to whoever was listening that his man understood him. He knew Boyd wouldn't out him and hated what his father was saying but he was frozen. Scared like a deer in a hunter's snare. He couldn't think. Turning back to the team as he led his father through the training area, he gave them all his best *I'm sorry* look and hoped they knew him well enough to know why.

Boyd hated Jørgensen Senior. Hearing Vidar's stories the night before, he already hated him but meeting the man in person, seeing and hearing his blatant homophobia and how he treated Vidar, made him want revenge.

As soon as the door to the training area closed, Boyd heard the eerie silence. Looking around at the team, Boyd saw the stunned looks.

"Did that really just happen?" Gabe asked.

"You know what they say. Never meet your idols, they'll always disappoint," Sweet said from beside him.

"Vi mentioned his father's... dislike of homosexuals before," Callum stated.

"Let him think it's just Rhys and me. If he knew we're a team made up of LGBT+ community members it would out him and we can't do that," Kiter ordered.

Gabe's father stood beside his grandsons and shook his head. "Shame on him. No father should be like that. Our role is to help our kids, not hurt and condemn them."

"Not everyone can be you, Dad," Gabe smiled lovingly at his father.

"Well, I don't know about you, but I'm not going to let this slide," Boyd said.

"Boyd, no," Rhys stepped forward. "You can't do anything without hurting him."

"Oh, there's plenty I can do without hurting him. And I never would, surly you know that." He turned to Nigel Sweet's mother. "Mama Sweet, can you help me?"

"Of course, darlin'," she agreed walking over. "That nasty man needs to be taught a lesson."

"Mama, I love you, but maybe it's not your place?" Nigel offered hesitantly.

"If not me, who?" She replied and walked with Boyd to his room.

Half an hour later, Mama Sweet clapped her hands with a giddy smile. "Knock 'em dead, baby," she said, and Boyd grinned.

Chapter Eleven

"**A**nd that brings us back to the beginning," Vidar said as he ended the tour for his father. Trying to keep his voice even, he decidedly did not think about how talking about his father last night with Boyd, had possibly conjured him.

"This is one hell of a gig, son," his father said. He shook his head. "Still not sure I like you being in such close quarters with a couple of fags."

"*Far,* please, that word is offensive."

"Not to us. We're no queers."

"Dad," he forced.

His father stopped walking and turned to look at him. Vidar tried not to squirm under his father's scrutiny. But he knew that look. As a boy, he'd try to run and hide if ever he saw that look.

"Why are you defending them? Why do you care so much?"

"Because I'm a good person, and they're my friends," Vidar justified.

"Friends," his father spat. "Make sure that's all it is."

"Would it be so horrible? If I was gay?" Vidar should have known, but he didn't expect his father to actually slap him. The sound of flesh striking flesh resounded in the area and the biting sting on his cheek bloomed. Vidar's mind finally caught up with the circumstance. He breathed out in shock.

"Never say those words. My son is *not* gay. Understand?"

"There you are," a soft feminine voice came from Vidar's right. He turned and froze. "I heard your dad was here. Silly, why didn't you tell me?"

Boyd, in full drag, make up, wig, heels, and tight jeans with a flowery top and earrings, saddled up to him. Vidar stared into the beautiful eyes of the man he spent the night with. The smoky eyeshadow, liner, and fake eyelashes rimmed his eye, Boyd's makeup was flawless yet tasteful enough that he made a very convincing woman. His willowy dancer physique helped, but from his dark roots and light hair wig to the five-inch heels he rocked, Boyd Falstaff looked stunning.

"Well hello, who's this?" Oskar sounded interested.

Boyd broke his gaze and gave the most winning smile he had to Vidar's father. "Lynette Falstaff, a pleasure to meet you, Mr. Jørgensen. Vidy didn't tell me you were here. I had to hear it from my brother."

"Your brother?" Oskar asked.

"Yes, you met him earlier, Agent Autolycus?"

"Oh, yes the young one."

"That's him," Boyd stroked his hand up and down Vidar's arm.

"How do you know my boy?" Oskar asked.

Boyd gave a soft gasp and turned to Vidar. "You naughty boy, you didn't tell your daddy about me?"

"Slipped my mind." Up to that moment, Vidar wasn't sure he would or could play along. But hearing the subtle *Daddy* in his words, Vidar couldn't stop himself. Boyd looked stunning and had done all this for him.

He loved him. The sudden realization was... not terrifying.

"That's what six months gets me? You'll pay for this tonight, baby," Boyd looked over to Vidar's father. "Vi and I have been dating for six months. We were hoping to get up to Norway to meet you but with the team just up and running, it was hard to get away."

"Oh, sweetheart, not to worry." The soft blush on his dad's cheeks made Vidar laugh. "You are beautiful."

"Oh," Boyd smiled and giggled prettily. "I am keeping you."

"Not sure how he got you," Oskar indicated Vidar.

"I'm the luckiest girl," Boyd said. "Vidar's such a gentleman, everywhere but the sheets." He leaned forward and whispered conspiratorially. "A beast, I tell you."

"Gets it from his father," Oskar wiggled his eyebrows.

"I don't doubt it," Boyd grinned.

"We're going to dinner tonight. You must join us," Oskar gushed.

"Oh sweetie, I wouldn't dream of it." Boyd shook his head.

"Please, I need to get to know my boy's girlfriend," Oskar tried.

"Still, I wish I could. But you two go and have fun. I

promise, next time."

"I'll hold you to that," he said.

"Far, don't you have to get going? It's nearly 0940," Vidar reminded him.

"Oh, is it? Shit. Well, this has definitely been one of the best visits," he said and opened his arms to Boyd. Boyd leaned forward and air kissed him on the cheeks.

"So wonderful to meet you. Vidy has told me very little of his childhood, but I've wanted to meet the people responsible for creating this gorgeous and amazing man so badly."

"Well, it's certainly wonderful to meet you. You sure make a cute couple," Oskar said. "You'll make I some beautiful babies."

Vidar choked on air and coughed. Boyd giggled. "We do love getting some practice in, don't we, baby?"

"That's my boy," Oskar cheered.

"I'll walk you out, Dad." Vidar extracted his arm from Boyd's hand.

"When you're done, you and Boyd need to meet up at the training area. Kiter told me to tell you," Boyd said.

"I'll be there," Vidar gave a wink that he hoped said everything he wanted and needed to say.

Boyd grinned and kissed him. For a brief moment, Vidar's heart felt like it stopped. He was kissing his boyfriend, dressed in drag, pretending to be his girlfriend, in front of his father. A small thrill raced through him.

When Boyd pulled back, he finger-waved to his dad and walked away, a definite swing in his hips. Oskar and Vidar watched him leave.

"Mm," Oskar grunted. "I tell you what... how the hell did you get her?"

"I'm best friends with her brother," he lied easily.

"A woman like that won't wait around, Vidar. You need to snatch her up and fast."

"I'll keep that in mind. Come on, you'll be late. Where are you staying? I can pick you up at 1830 for dinner."

With the exchange of information, Vidar escorted his father back to the main area where the team waited. Gabe's boys and parents, and Nigel's parents had left the area. Vidar heard squealing laughter when he passed the door to the pool.

"Leaving so soon?" Kiter questioned.

Oskar sneered at him. "It was a pleasure meeting most of you. Where's Lynette?"

"She's getting things ready in the training room," Gabe explained, and Vidar saw he was trying to hide his smirk.

"Everything's set," Lynette's voice came from the hallway and Boyd saddled up beside Vidar. "Don't think I was going to let you leave without a proper goodbye."

"Hoped not," Oskar winked and gave Boyd a kiss on the cheek. "See you again soon, sweetheart."

"You can bet on it," Boyd replied.

Vidar called for the lift and as soon as the doors opened, Oskar got in and held up a hand stopping Vidar from entering. "I've taken up too much of your time already. You have things to do. I can find my own way. I'm proud of you, Vi. See you tonight." The doors shut and Vidar let out a breath while Gabe and Rhys let out their laugh. Wheezing, they started clapping for Boyd who took a bow, then another.

"Thank you, thank you, I'll be by to pick up my Academy Award later tonight," Boyd said.

"Ms. Lynette, if you could let your *brother* know we could

use him in training, that would be great," Kiter teased.

"I'll think about." With a wink, Boyd turned back to the room and blew Vidar a kiss as he disappeared into his room.

"Did that really just happen?" Vidar asked. Kiter and Rhys turned back to him with silly grins.

"Yes, it did," Kiter said.

"My father just met my boyfriend posing as my girlfriend, and I kiss him... her... in front of him..."

The room was silent, and Vidar remembered his words, wincing.

"*Boyfriend,* is it?" Rhys asked then turned to his husband. "See Somm, this is what happens when you let the boys go home for a few hours. They wake the hell up and we can all stop pussy-footin' around." Rhys slapped Vidar on the back.

"Guess those nonfraternization agreements are moot now, huh?" Kiter asked.

"They were moot the second you were in my bed, baby," Rhys said.

"Guess that's true," Kiter acquiesced.

"But seriously, it's about time," Gabe said from beside Nigel in his wheelchair. "We're happy for you, Vi."

"Thank you. It's really new, but it's been... eye opening."

"Of course it has," Nigel replied. "There's nothing quite like getting the love of your life." He looked lovingly up at his fiancé beside him as Rhys and Kiter agreed, sharing a soft kiss.

"Not sure I want to ask, but I guess it's an improvement from walking in on bawdy comments about male appendages," Marjorie's voice came from the lift.

"Morning, Marge," Kiter greeted. "Just discussing the uselessness of the fraternization docs."

"Oh, I shredded those weeks ago," she winked. "Congrats, Vidar."

Vidar was taken aback. "What? How did you know?"

Marjorie tapped the side of her nose as she stepped further into the room. "Anymore coffee? I've been dreaming about it all morning."

"In the pot," Nigel offered. "Mama and Papa brought over a dozen bags. They know it's my favorite."

"I understand," she agreed and grabbed a mug. "So, what's good? What's going on?"

"You'll never believe it." Rhys laughed again and the team launched into the story.

Vidar tuned them out, his thoughts only on Boyd and the dinner with his father. But soon, Boyd emerged from his room, back to his usual looking self and Vidar's heartbeat ticked higher. He was beautiful, but he was all his man and he loved it. Boyd grinned, grabbed a mug of coffee, and slid up beside him.

"You were brilliant," Vidar whispered.

"That arse had it coming. After what you went through, I couldn't stop myself. He messed with my man and I protect what's mine."

The corner of Vidar's lip ticked up as he looked down at him. "And am I?"

"Are you what?" Boyd asked.

"Yours."

Boyd set the mug of coffee down and cradled Vidar's head in both hands, forcing him to look at him. "You better believe it, Thor. You're mine. Always." Then Boyd's lips were on his and Vidar melted as the team erupted in cheers.

Chapter Twelve

Mission Accomplished.

The green light flashed throughout the training room again for the third time that day. Boyd jumped into Vidar's arms and sloppily kissed him in celebration. He found he couldn't stop kissing him or feeling his hands on his body. The team came over and slapped them both on the back in excitement.

"So when are we doing this?" Boyd asked Kiter who took a deep breath.

"Soon. But let's keep at this first. I'm not willing to go on a potentially high stakes mission with only five accomplished run throughs. But—" he held up his hand when Boyd began to protest. "I think it's time we get a better look at the area. So, Collins, Sweet, think you can *play dumb* and get a good look at the area?"

"Yeah," Gabe agreed. "With Sweet still in the wheelchair, it will help."

Boyd lowered his feet to the floor as Vidar set him down. "I need to be there. I'm the one going in. I should be able to see it."

"I don't want to risk them recognizing you," Kiter said. "Collins and Sweet will wear body cams. You can see it virtually."

Boyd shook his head. "You know I'm right, boss. I need to do this."

Kiter paused and took a deep breath. "Fine. But you sit in the wheelchair. And no, Vidar, you aren't going with him. The less you two are seen together upstairs, the easier it will be."

Boyd heard Vidar grind his teeth. Slipping his hand into Vidar's, Boyd squeezed. "Then who?"

"Callum, you up for it? We need to be stealthy," Kiter asked their team leader.

Callum looked up and Boyd's gaze zeroed into Callum's eyes. The circles ringing his eyes but were darker than usual and the haunted look in his eyes made Boyd shiver. Callum stared at Kiter as if they were having their own conversation.

Then, without words to Callum, Kiter turned to Gabe. "You're up."

Gabe's brow furrowed and his eyes went from Kiter to Callum, then back. "Sure."

"Good, let's get you geared up."

It took less than twenty minutes for Gabe and Boyd to get mic'd and body cammed. Vidar wrapped Boyd's leg with a bandage to make it more believable as he sat in Nigel's wheelchair.

Nigel sat propped on the couch, his broken and crushed legs still in their cast but a smile on his face as he played cards with Gabe's boys, his godsons.

"Now, no one is to play hero. You feel they're getting suspicious; you leave. You need extraction, you call for it, understand?" Kiter said.

"We got this, boss," Boyd answered.

Gabe walked over from where he was talking to his boys and Nigel. He grabbed the handles of the wheelchair and nodded once at Kiter. "Boyd's right. We got this."

"I know you do, still be careful," Kiter cautioned. "We'll be on comms."

The lift doors opened and Vi, Kiter, and Callum entered heading up to the offices to listen and watch on comms. Rhys stayed with the families and Sweet. When Gabe called the lift again, Boyd took a deep breath focusing his mind.

The doors opened. "Ready?" Gabe asked.

"Ready."

Gabe wheeled them into the lift and turned around. Before the doors closed, Boyd saw the look in Sweet's eyes as he stared at his fiancé. He was worried.

A simple recon should be easy, but one thing Boyd learned at that job was, nothing was easy. And anything could go wrong.

The back hall was quiet on the main floor as Gabe wheeled Boyd down the corridor to the lifts securing the basement. Boyd's eyes bounced back and forth, up and down and for a moment his stomach pitched. He wished he could see Gabe. There was something comforting about seeing another agent. But Gabe stayed behind him, pushing the wheelchair.

"Scorpio, do you read?" Boyd whispered.

"Affirmative, Autolycus, loud and clear," he heard over the earpieces.

"Approaching lift."

"Understood. Mission is go."

"Auto, this is Mamabear," Marjorie's voice came next. "I'll guide you through."

"Understood, Mamabear, heading into lift now."

It was so quiet inside the lift, but Boyd and Gabe knew better than to speak. Nearly everywhere in MI6 HQ was mic'd and covered in CCTV cameras, some unseen. Boyd's eyes were on the numbers going down. The vault was in Sub-Basement 9 and the infirmary was in Sub-Basement 6, which was an easy mistake to wave off if they got caught.

The bell dinged and Boyd felt Gabe's hand on his shoulder giving it a squeeze. It helped settle him as the doors opened.

And they were faced with three armed guards aiming weapons at their faces.

"Uh," Boyd breathed, eyes bouncing back and forth between the guards as they all shouted orders at them.

"Stand down," a forceful voice came from behind the men. The guns were lowered, and the commander stepped forward. "Boyd?" He questioned.

"Dae-Hyun?" Boyd asked seeing the Korean man he had met in Vidar's flat the night before.

"What are you doing here? Are you all right?" He rushed toward him looking at his leg.

"Oh... yeah, just twisted my ankle and landed on my knee. We were looking for infirmary," Boyd answered.

"Up three floors. SB6."

"Right," Boyd nodded as Gabe called the lift. "Thanks."

"Is Vi with you?" Dae asked side-eying Gabe behind him.

"Yeah, he's upstairs. Reaper was kind enough to offer to take me. We must have hit the wrong button."

Dae's eyes twitched but he nodded slowly. "SB9 is restricted. Only cleared agents can enter, hence," he motioned to his team.

"I thought you retired," Boyd said remembering when they dropped Sheila off with Gareth that morning.

"From Active Military Duty, yes, but Gareth has his hobbies, and they were recruiting for security. Don't have clearance for higher up but it works."

"Private contractors?" Gabe asked.

Dae's shrewd eyes moved up to stare at Gabe. "Something like that. Bunch of old military guys needing the thrill, you know."

The twin lift dinged, and the team turned toward it.

"Woah, what the hell?" Boyd recognized Vidar's surprised voice.

"Stand down," Dae looked over. "Vi? What's going on?"

"Dae? I could ask you the same thing." Vidar stepped out of the lift and turned to Boyd. "Baby, there you are. I got worried. I looked for you in infirm, but you weren't there. Figured you might have hit the wrong button."

"Must have," Boyd replied. Vidar stepped into the elevator with Boyd and Gabe when their doors opened.

"Let's get you looked at. Dae, I'll not ask what you're doing here but we need to catch up. Let's get lunch in half an hour?" Vidar asked.

Dae nodded slowly. "I can do that."

"Great!" Vidar forced. "Meet you at Rocketman around the corner?"

Dae nodded again, his eyes following Vidar as the doors to the lift closed. The silence was tense as they rode the lift back up, walked down the hall, and got to the bunker. Once the doors opened, they saw Kiter pacing and Marjorie sitting nervously on one of the high-top stools by the kitchen. The rest of the team stood or sat around the main room. Their family members gave them the privacy they needed.

Kiter turned to them as soon as they stepped out. Boyd, foregoing the wheelchair, walked over to Marjorie to give her comfort. "That's new," she said. "There weren't guards at the lift two weeks ago."

"It's okay. It's just an added layer we need to prep for," Boyd assured.

"Vidar," Kiter spoke. "Do you think Lee will work with us?"

"If we make a case, yes. He's as loyal as they come but explain and read him in on all of it, he'll become our best asset. He's black and white when it comes to serving his country, but he hates corruption," Vidar explained.

"And Godwin?" Kiter asked after Dae's husband.

"What about him?"

"Can he keep it from him? Or do we need to recruit them both?" Kiter asked.

"Dae is confidential."

"How do you know them, boss?" Boyd asked.

"I was colonel over their SRR. In a way, Lee, Godwin, and Vidar worked for me," Kiter explained. "Bring Lee here after lunch. We need to know what he knows. Why the new security?"

"Could they have gotten a whiff of something?" Callum

asked.

"They must have," Rhys agreed. "But how? No accusations, but did anyone say anything? To anyone?"

Various murmurs of *no* and *I didn't* went around the room. Eyes turned to Kiter when he didn't speak.

"Somm?" Rhys asked.

"Lester had me discuss our current mission load with the Deputy Secretary, his boss. I mentioned nothing about what we planned but I noticed the Deputy Secretary's assistant watching our run through the other day. One of the failed attempts. Lester was with him. The assistant may have noticed the similarity."

Silence descended on the team as the seriousness of Kiter's statement took hold in their minds.

"Are you saying this corruption goes up to the Deputy Secretary?" Nigel questioned.

"I'm saying the assistant saw what we were doing. I have no proof of anything else," Kiter said. "But this has changed things."

"Let me talk to Dae," Vidar spoke up. "He'll listen. Trust me."

Kiter nodded. "Very well. Let's reconvene at 1500. Bring Dae if you're convinced of his loyalty."

"I will," Vidar swore and with a longing look at Boyd, headed to the lift to meet Dae at the pub around the corner. Boyd sent all his hope and confidence his way and blew him a kiss as the door shut.

Chapter Thirteen

Vidar entered the pub and quickly found Dae at the bar top, a beer in hand talking to the keeper. He walked over and slid onto the stool beside him, slapping Dae on the back in greeting.

"Heya," Dae returned. Then, turning to the pubkeeper, continued. "Arlo, this is my friend Vidar."

"Oh, I know this one," Arlo teased with his upper London accent. "What can I get you, Vi?"

"I haven't ordered food yet," Dae explained.

"I'll do a wheat and today's special," Vidar replied seeing the ham and cheese sandwich with chips. Arlo acknowledged and began pouring the beer as he spoke to Dae.

"And for you, handsome?"

"Special is good for me too, Ar, cheers," Dae answered. "This place is great," Dae spoke to Vidar. "I can't believe you've never invited Gare and me here."

"It's fun at night too," Vidar answered as Arlo placed his beer in front of him. "Cheers, Arlo." He continued to Dae. "It changes into a nightclub with drag shows, dancers, and comedy gigs."

"Always looking for more acts too. You dance?" Arlo asked Dae.

"No," he chuckled. "My sister-in-law is the dancer of the family."

"Pity, you'd rake in the cash, handsome," Arlo said.

"Ooh, hubby wouldn't like it."

"Eh, he'd probably be the highest payer," winking Arlo tapped the top of the bar and turned. "I'll get your orders in."

Once they were alone, Dae took a slow swig of his beer, staring ahead.

"Wanna head to the snug?" Vidar offered.

Dae offered a forced, no-teeth smile. "Sure." Then, catching Arlo's attention as he made his way back from putting their orders in, said, "could I get another one of these?"

"Sure thing."

"We'll be in the snug, Ar," Vidar said, slipping off the stool and following a clip behind Dae to the small, semiprivate room.

Sitting opposite each other with a small square table between them, Dae leaned back, glanced out the open archway to the rest of the pub, which was quiet, and then pinned Vidar with a look that had his heart pounding.

"Wanna tell me what the fuck is going on? And why does the CCB want to get into the vaults my team and I are charged with protecting? And why you and Boyd lied to my damn face?"

Vidar took a deep breath, and a sip of his beer. With the alcoholic fortitude he needed, he began. "You always like things out in the open, Dae. I'm sorry to have lied to you. I wasn't sure if we could trust those around you. There's a traitor in MI6." Vidar let the words sink in and watched Dae's face for a reaction.

Dae schooled his features and tapped his manicured nails on the table. "Go on."

"The first mission the boys ever went on, they lost two agents. It was one of the reasons I was recruited. The mission was supposed to be a simple extraction, nothing we haven't done ourselves thousands of times. But someone tipped off the Rentai Cartel and they got there first."

Dae frowned. "Rentai... the Yakuza affiliate?"

"The same."

Dae took a breath. "You're lucky you have a team."

"I know. But someone contacted them from inside HQ."

"And you have proof of that?" Dae asked.

"Not as much," Vidar answered. "But process of elimination, it was someone with connections. Someone who knew our mission parameters. And someone who could give the order."

"Could have just been sloppy intel. Or could have been the mark had pissed off the Japanese mafia and needed elimination."

"Could have, yes. But why then, are we constantly given bad intel? We were in—" Vidar stopped speaking when Arlo walked up with two plates and a beer for Dae. Seeming to realize he was interrupting something, he said nothing and patted Vi on the shoulder as he left. Vidar waited until he was out of earshot. "We were in Transylvania a little over two weeks ago. Agent

Oleksandr Demidov or Sasha as he went by, was our contact. He caused an accident for one of my teammates. Nearly killed him. He also killed another agent a few years ago. He was the contact for the FSB and our agent was sent in to see if she could find why ten of our agents in and around Russia had their covers blown and were killed. She was in the process of uploading evidence of Sasha's involvement when he shot her in the back. She was on comms with her handler and wife."

Dae took a breath, paused, then spoke again. "And your evidence of that?"

"Testimony by the wife, her handler. Testimony of my teammate who Sasha shot as well as a recorded conversation on voicemail. Evidence of meetings between Sasha and a man named Kyetti. He's an international war criminal specializing in drug and sex trafficking. He confirmed Sasha was working for him, but he is in the wind. Some solicitor got him out of MI6 custody and when he was found floating in the Thames, Kyetti was nowhere to be found. That vault is our link to Kyetti's and Sasha's involvement. We don't know what's in it, but why else would they be protecting it with your team, extra guards, lasers, infrared, and possible biometrics? Our team is being targeted by someone for some reason. We need to know if the contents of that vault are enough to take to the higher ups."

"How do you know you can trust the higher ups?"

"We don't. That's what we're hoping to discover."

Dae was quiet for a long moment. "Are you prepared for the consequences of this? You fail, you are a traitor and everything you've done in your life and military career will be scrutinized and by extension, us; Geoff, me, Team Alice." He mentioned their SRR team name. "You will be stripped of your rank, and they will send men, like our team, possibly even your former brothers in SRR, to kill you and Boyd and everyone else on CCB. And if I help you, it's my life, my career, Gare's life and career. I can't risk it."

"And what happens if we don't fail?" Vidar asked. "What happens if we find the traitor, have the evidence, and get them behind bars? What happens if we don't do this? Who knows how close to the king this person is. Are you really willing to risk the monarchy for a possible?"

"Don't pull the love of the monarchy on me, you know they're not my favorite people. I'm loyal because I'm a British citizen but I'm no loyalist. Don't confuse the two. But that said. I took an oath to the crown, and I will protect it. However, I don't like the idea of being blacklisted." He huffed a sigh.

Vidar watched Dae-Hyun's face. He had served by Vidar's side in Afghanistan, Iraq, and Libya. He and Gareth were his best friends. If Vidar lost them, he wasn't sure what he would do.

"You will do this with or without my help, won't you?" Dae asked.

"Yes," the answer was simple.

"And possibly get yourself killed in the process."

"If I can protect Boyd, save the team, expose the corruption, it would be worth it."

Dae sighed again. "Well... we can't have that," he said then nodded slowly. "I've got your six."

Vidar breathed easier and smiled for the first time since coming into the pub. "Thank you."

The corner of Dae's lip tipped up. "You're my brother... our brother," he said. "I can't let you do this alone." The mood shifted with Dae's smile. "Telling me all of this, does this mean I'm an honorary member of your little group?"

"You want a sticker or something?" Vidar teased.

"That'd be nice," Dae laughed and turned his attention to the lunch before him.

They ate in companionable silence for a short moment before, "my dad's in town," Vidar dropped.

Dae nearly spat out his food. "What?" He questioned around a bite of sandwich.

Vidar nodded. "Surprised me by showing up at the office today."

Dae stared at him and swallowed his food. "Arlo," he gained the barkeeper's attention and lifted his half full glass. "Another round please." Once he nodded, Dae turned back to Vidar. "We're going to need it. You told him where you work?"

"He's my emergency contact. I had to."

"I'm hurt," Dae said. "Could have used us."

"Had to be blood, if I had any."

"So what happened?" Dae asked.

"He just showed up. I dropped Sheila off with Gare this morning and Boyd and I drove in. I thought I might die when the doors opened. I was holding Boyd in my arms."

Dae's eyes widened. "Did he see you?"

"No, thankfully. But when he met Kiter and his husband, he began spouting the usual blather about how he doesn't like me hanging out with gays and how his son will never and could never like anything other than pussy, all while I could still taste my boyfriend's lip gloss in my mouth and feel his body in my arms."

Arlo clicked his tongue in disapproval as he placed the beer on the table. "There's one in every family. My entire extended family have never met my husband." Arlo gave him a sympathetic pat on the shoulder and left them alone.

"I've heard your dad's homophobic bullshit. I'm sorry you had to hear it so early in your realization. Did you tell him? About you and Boyd?" Dae asked.

Vidar shook his head as he dragged one of the chips through ketchup and popped it into his mouth. "No, I couldn't. Not right then. And later," he let out a breathy laugh. "Boyd dressed in drag and pretended to be my girlfriend."

Dae stared then burst out laughing. "Are you serious?" Then, he stopped and thought for a moment. Nodding, "I could see it. He'd make a very convincing woman. Your dad fell for it?"

"Hook, line, and sinker. Told me not to make a good woman like that wait and we'd make some beautiful babies."

Dae covered his mouth so his beer wouldn't spew out of his mouth as he laughed. "I would have paid a high price to see that and the look on your dad's face when he finds out *she* is a *he.*"

Vidar went quiet and took a drink. Dae observed him.

"Vi? You are going to tell him, right?" Dae asked. Vidar stayed quiet. "You owe it to yourself and Boyd if you're serious about him. Believe me, I know how scary it is. Korean parents and an only child? It's not easy to admit when you love a man as a man. All the heteronormativity that surrounds us every day makes it so tough to be vulnerable. But believe me, it's so worth it. Yeah, my dad didn't speak to me for six months, even told me I wasn't his son anymore, but my mother tried. She *tried* and that's what mattered. My father came around and accepted me back, but I told him *I'm still gay* and he hugged me. My father doesn't hug. It's not exactly the same as before, but he *tries.* And it's heartwarming to see him treating Gare like a son. He even introduces him as his *sawi.* He introduces him as his *son-in-law,* Vi," he stressed. "The first time I saw him show Gare how to fold *Mandu,* I nearly cried.

My dad had accepted him in his own way. It was perfect. And now they go to football games together like a father and son-in-law. Hell, my parents gave me away at my wedding."

"I know, I was there," Vi answered. "But Dae, my dad's not like your dad. He will kill me."

"You think I didn't think my dad would kill me, too?" Dae questioned then reached across the table and covered Vidar's hand with his. "You have every right to feel that way. I've not gone what you have with your father. But if not for him, do it for yourself. You owe yourself that much. He's been controlling you your whole life. Even when he has no power over you. He's controlling you, like now. You're thinking of what *he* would want. That's not fair to you. I love you like a brother, Vi. I don't like seeing you like this. Stand up against that narcissist once and for all. If that means you lose him, so be it.

"What would you rather have? A man who will never and has never let you be yourself? A bully who physically abused you, put you in the hospital then mentally punished you if you didn't act a certain way? Someone you have run from your entire adult life... or a man who cares for you, dare say loves you. Someone who wants you for you. To be with you. Cares about your thoughts, feelings, someone who wants to help you become the man he knows exists. Who would you rather have? Your father? Or Boyd? I know who I'd pick."

Dae held his gaze for a long moment before squeezing his hand and pulling back. They ate in silence and soon their food dwindled, and their beer foamed the bottom of the glass. It was time to head out. But Vidar felt a little guilty. "I haven't asked how you and Gareth are doing. I feel like I dumped so much on you the last two days. I'm sorry I haven't asked."

117

"We're fantastic as usual," Dae answered. "It was funny, yesterday when we got home without Sheila, he drew us a bath. She always wants to get in with us, so it was nice not to have her there," he winked.

Vidar blushed. "You and your baths and showers. I swear..."

"Don't hate, just because you've caught us and will now forever have that mental image in your head... you're welcome, by the way," Dae beamed. "But his birthday is coming up and I asked him what he wanted. You know what that gorgeous man said?"

"Am I going to regret asking?"

"Probably," he chuckled. "A threesome."

"And you agreed?" Vidar lifted an eyebrow.

"Wouldn't be the first," he teased. "And there's something really hot about seeing him rail some bloke as I take him."

"Image!"

"You're welcome," Dae drained his beer, grinning.

"Jesus, I didn't need that in my head."

"You know, you're going to have to get out of your comfort zone with that man of yours. Boyd doesn't strike me as a vanilla sex kind of guy. More like really hot, *hot* kinky sex."

"Get the thought of my boyfriend as the third bloke in your scenario out of your head. He's mine and I don't share well."

Dae leaned back in the chair, his empty beer glass still in his hand, watching him. "You know..." he drawled. "That's the second time you've said that."

"Said what?"

"Boyfriend."

Vidar swallowed. "So?"

"So is it true? Is Boyd your boyfriend? Because Gare and I

really like him for you."

Vidar looked away. "Yeah, it's true, at least for me. I haven't really asked him to be my boyfriend. I sort of just assumed."

The corner of Dae's lip tipped up. "Sometime that's the best."

"Sometimes." Vidar made a mental note to ask Boyd to be his boyfriend as soon as he got back to HQ.

"So," Dae pinned him with a knowing grin. "More things happened after Gare and I left, huh?"

"Yeah," Vi agreed. "But we just made out. We didn't... didn't."

"Have sex?" Dae prompted.

"Yeah."

"You didn't?"

"Yeah, didn't."

"What the hell are you waiting for, idiot?" Dae questioned.

"It's a big step for me, okay?" Vidar sighed.

Dae was quiet for a long moment then, leaning forward, he whispered. "Oh my god, is this your first guy?"

Vidar glanced toward the entry to the snug. "Obviously."

"Oh ho, my god," Dae grinned. "Gareth owes me fifty quid."

"What?"

"He said you've been with a guy before. I knew you hadn't. Thanks for the money."

"You bet on me? Dae-Hyun Lee, you're supposed to be my best friend." Vidar stared.

"That's why it was fifty and not twenty," he winked.

"Oh my god," Vidar wiped his hand down his face.

"No seriously, that answers so many questions," Dae went on. "Have you... ever? With a woman?"

"Of course! I'm not..." Vidar searched for the word he was trying to think of.

"A virgin?"

"A recluse," he stated. "But it's never been... I don't know. I honestly thought I was more asexual or demi before I met Boyd."

"Look at you, throwing big identities out there."

Vidar gave him a pointed look. "I researched. Any time I was with a woman, it wasn't satisfying," Vidar admitted. "I've felt more pleasure with Boyd in the simple kisses we shared than in all of my experiences."

"Hmm," Dae nodded. "You probably never let yourself relax enough. You were only doing it to show your dad you weren't gay. You want my advice?"

"Can I stop you?"

"Of course," Dae answered honestly.

"Tell me."

"Do something spontaneous. Something fun he will like. Get out of your comfort zone. You've sat by for too long. Something that puts you out there, but just for him. Think about his pastimes and hobbies. Do something like that for him. Get into his sports teams... unless it's Liverpool then I will disown you as a friend."

"Spoken like a true Arsenal fan," Vidar chuckled.

"I'm serious, Vi. I can forgive a lot. Liverpool fan? Never."

"Understood," he smiled.

"You'll figure something out and I know he'll love it. It will also show him you're interested in his hobbies. I got into cars for Gare. I honestly couldn't care less about them. So long as they had four wheels and an engine to get me from one place to the other, I really didn't care. But Gare's obsessed and I found a couple books on them, studied, and took him to a car show for our one-year anniversary and surprised him with my knowledge. Trust me," a salacious grin spread across Dae's mouth and Vidar chuckled. "It works. And we've made it a yearly thing. It's actually pretty fun."

"I have something in mind," Vidar said. "Could you help me?"

"Whatever I can do."

"Do you have Gareth's sister's number?"

It took Dae a second, but realization dawned, and he pulled out his phone. "Now I'm curious. Why would you need a West End choreographer's number?"

Vidar tapped the side of his nose as he heard his phone ding with Dae's text. "Tell her to expect my call?"

"Put you in a group text already. I'm her favorite brother-in-law so she usually texts back pretty quickly," Dae boasted.

"Aren't you her only brother-in-law?"

"Still favorite."

Vidar chuckled. After a beat, looking down at their nearly empty plates, he pulled back from the table. "Ready? I'd like you to come back with me to the team."

"Yeah, let's head back."

Saying bye to Arlo with a promise they'd all come back by soon and he'd meet Dae's husband, they headed across the street to HQ. Arriving in the bunker, the team turned to look at them. Boyd instantly walked over to them.

"Hi, Dae-Hyun," he said. "Good to see you again."

"You too, Boyd, and feel free to call me Dae."

"Thanks," Boyd slipped his arm around Vidar and leaned into him as Dae greeted the rest of the team.

"Lee, good to see you again," Kiter said.

"You as well, Colonel. Vidar read me in. What can I do to

help?"

"Think you could watch our sim and see if it works with your understanding of the location?" Kiter asked.

"Point me in the right direction."

"Follow me," Sweet called from the wheelchair. "Everyone else is part of the sim. You can hang out with me in the observation deck."

"Sounds good." With a glance back at Vidar, Dae followed.

"We'll be right there, boss," Vidar said holding Boyd back.

Boyd looked up at him, questioningly. "What's up?"

"I – ehm – wanted to ask you something."

"All right," Boyd rested his arms over Vidar's shoulders. Vidar held him close. "What is it? I can feel your nerves."

"I'm a bit nervous. I don't know if I'm rushing this, please tell me if I am. But... I just sort of assumed and I realize now, I shouldn't have. I mean, maybe it's okay. But I should have asked you before I just assumed and said something to everyone. But see, I've never been in this position, so I don't know what's normal or what to expect and I don't want to do anything to jeopardize us, and I just feel like—"

"Yes."

Vidar stopped abruptly at the interruption. "What?"

"My answer is yes. I will be your boyfriend, Vidar. Thank you for asking."

Vidar let out a laugh and crushed Boyd to his chest. "Thank you, boyfriend... that's silly. Sorry that was really silly."

Boyd's tinkling laugh filled him with warmth. "You're welcome, boyfriend. I did like seeing you floundering. It was cute, like a baby deer and for a man your size, it was adorable."

"Baby deer?"

"Mmhmm," Boyd grinned, and Vidar lifted him up in his arms. Boyd wrapped his legs around Vidar's waist and held on. Their lips met and Vidar was sure he saw fireworks, heard bells, and felt a sort of lightning. Everything *they* say you're supposed to feel when you fall for someone."

Chapter Fourteen

Boyd stood with Vidar in their debriefing room after two run throughs of the sim. Kiter was explaining what they did well and what could still use improvement as they watched themselves on the projector screen. When Kiter finished, Boyd's eyes drifted to the wall clock. Vidar needed to get ready to meet his father for dinner soon.

"It's getting close to 1700," Boyd whispered in Vidar's ear. Giving him a confused look, Vidar glanced at the clock then back. "You need to pick up your dad for dinner soon."

Vidar's face skewed up in disgust but nodded and turned back to Kiter.

"All right, Boys, listen up," Kiter's voice rang through the room. "I'm going to pass this off to Lee for some advice then let's run it again."

"Boss," Vidar spoke up. "Can I head out around 1745? I have to pick up my dad for dinner."

Boyd noticed the look on Dae's face when he said that, but Kiter nodded. "Of course, yeah. Lee?" Kiter turned to him.

"I'm pleased to be here to help you all. My experience with this vault area is little over two weeks so I've seen every rotation but that's not infallible. So, there are three teams of four guards at the entrance of the lift at all times except between 2100 and 0400. That's our window of opportunity. The four guards within the vault area are twenty-four-seven. However, during the down times as you know there are lasers and infrared. My recommendation would be to not go through the lift. Even the shaft had cameras at that time of day. There is a maintenance hatch here," Dae showed on the screen and zoomed in.

"That will lead you here. This hatch opens into the storage room. That room is always kept locked with only the Chief Maintenance Officer in possession of the key. But it can be easily picked from the other side." He glanced at Boyd who nodded, giddy he had a new opportunity. "That will lead you out here," Dae showed where the first round of lasers lit the ground and walls. "Then, it's home free until you get here," he pointed at the vault. "The door is much more complicated than I think you realize. The one you have for practice is easy. There are a lot of more details, not to mention it's a heavy ass door. I figured you're strong Boyd, but it takes two guards to open it."

"I'll be with him," Vidar said.

"Then who has your six?" Dae questioned. "You are supposed to be watching him, you turn away, who watches for you? Just a thought. I'm on shift again in two days, I'll try to get some images of the vault for you, Boyd but it won't be easy. You'll have to bear with me and be patient. It could take some time so as to not draw suspicion."

"We have the time but not a lot," Kiter said. "We'd rather you be safe than risk rushing anything and getting someone hurt."

"Agreed," Dae stated. "So until then, the rest of the sim will translate well into the real thing. I'd say they've done a good job, Colonel."

Kiter smiled and slapped Dae on the back. "We owe you, Lee."

"Just promise me, you'll catch this arsehole who's threatening my country and friends."

"It's a promise I'm happy to make," Kiter said. "Now, I'd like to run through the sim once more and we can build the maintenance hatch portion of the sim tomorrow. After this, Vi you can head on out."

"Thanks, but I can cancel, if it's too much trouble," Vidar offered.

"Don't you dare," Boyd replied stopping him from grabbing his phone. Turning to Kiter, he continued. "I can help build part of it tonight, boss."

"I can stay too," Callum offered. "Not sleeping anyway."

"Maybe another hour after the sim but we'll want to get home. You're welcome to stay here, but Rhys and I haven't been home for a few days. I promised dinner and a movie," Kiter winked at his husband.

"We were hoping for a little change of scenery too, boss," Gabe piped up from beside Sweet. "Mum and Dad were going to take the boys to a hotel and Sweets and I were hoping to head home."

"Sounds good. But we can't let being home distract us from the still very real threat of Sasha. He knows where we all live and it's safe to say, he might have surveillance on us. Be vigilant and aware at all times. We'll see you back here tomorrow at 0800."

Rhys cleared his throat softly. "Somm," he whispered, as if reminding him of something. Kiter's brow furrowed as Rhys attempted to communicate with him silently. Kiter still didn't understand, and Rhys rolled his eyes. Leaning into whisper something, Rhys' voice was too low for Boyd to hear but Kiter's face went red, and his eyes widened, then a smirk lifted his lips.

"Right, let's try 1030 tomorrow, sleep in and have fun," he wiggled his brows suggestively and the men chuckled.

"If only," Nigel grumbled good-naturedly from his chair.

"There's still lots we can do, baby," Gabe kissed his cheek.

"Let's do a quick run through and then Vi, get on out of here."

Once the green light of Mission Accomplished lit the area, Vidar headed to the showers. The curtain opened as he lathered his body. Turning quickly, his tongue stuck to the top of his mouth when he saw Boyd, naked and glistening in the spray of water.

"I couldn't wait any longer to see you naked," Boyd teased. "And my god, I've never been so happy to claim all this as mine." He reached out and flattened his hands against Vidar's stomach which clenched at the touch. Boyd's hands were hot, and Vidar turned to face him.

"I really don't want to go to dinner," Vidar said. "I want to take you home and feed you, while I worship your body."

Boyd looked up at him. "Well, damn, you got a little bolder after your lunch with Dae. Remind me to thank him for whatever mind juju he pulled on you."

Vidar laughed and pulled Boyd to him. Their wet skin slipped and slid over each other's as their lips pressed together.

"I've jerked off so many times in this shower thinking about you," Vidar confessed between heated kisses.

"Show me," Boyd begged. "Show me how I make you come in your dreams."

Vidar pulled back and stared at him. Dae's words of getting out of his comfort zone rang in his ears. He decided then, he wasn't going to hide anything of himself from Boyd. As scary as it was, and it was scary as fuck, he was going to give him all of himself. Whatever he could. Starting with taking himself in hand and stroking steadily. He watched Boyd watching his hand and felt an addictive kind of power when Boyd's cheeks flushed. He made grabby hands toward Vidar's cock and Vi stepped back.

"Did Daddy say you could touch, boy?"

Boyd's eyes shot up to his. Searching his face, Boyd licked his lips. "Please, Daddy? I just want to feel it."

"No, be a good boy and watch. This is how I want to see you."

"Can I get on my knees for you? Paint my face with your cum, Daddy."

Vidar bit back a groan. "On your knees, baby boy," he said, unsure where his bravado was coming from. He'd never played a Daddy role for any of his hookups or long-term relationships. But something about Boyd made him want to.

Boyd slipped to his knees quickly and looked up at Vidar through his lashes. Face flushed, skin smooth and wet, dark hair dripping in his eyes, his cock prominent between his legs. It didn't take Vidar long, but fortunately he didn't embarrass himself by coming within twenty seconds as he was worried he might, but still it wasn't easy to hold out for longer.

"Can I touch your legs, Daddy?" Boyd asked so sweetly. "Hold on to you?"

"Yes," Vidar panted and as soon as Boyd's soft hands touched his thighs, his slim fingers digging in, holding him close, Vidar lost it. He came on a groan, slapping his free hand out to the side of the shower, the move familiar. He watched as Boyd opened his mouth catching some of his cum on his tongue. He moaned like it was the best thing he'd ever tasted, as some landed on his chin, forehead, cheeks, and hair. The sounds Boyd made and the image of how he looked covered in cum, Vidar's cum, extended Vidar's orgasm. He stroked himself until he winced, panting, his body loose, warm, and sated.

"Please," Boyd panted. "Please, Daddy, let me warm your cock."

Vidar thought he understood what he meant but wasn't prepared for what Boyd did. As soon as he nodded, Boyd leaned forward and scooped up the head into his mouth, holding it just inside his lips as his hand furiously stroked his own leaking cock. Vidar's back hit the tile as he felt the warmth of Boyd's tongue faintly caress the underside glans. Boyd's breathing picked up even more as his hand furiously pumped his cock, the tip nearly purple with need. He looked up, his eyes silently begging Vidar and only then did he realize what Boyd needed.

"Such a good boy," he cooed reaching out and stroking his fingers through Boyd's wet hair. "Let go, Daddy'll catch you. Come for me, baby," he ordered, and Boyd did. Letting loose a groan around Vidar's spent cock, Boyd came with a force that wracked his body. The sight, sounds, and feeling were almost too much for Vidar and he felt his cock twitch, attempting to get hard again. At thirty-six it was nearly impossible that quickly, but his body didn't seem to care. Still, Boyd fell forward, burying his forehead in the crease of Vidar's hip. He gave a soft moan when Vidar slipped his twitching cock out of his mouth and crouched down to hold him. Boyd went willingly, like a cat, into his arms, snuggling his head into the crook of Vidar's neck. "Such a good boy."

Boyd hummed and kissed his neck softly. "You got this," he whispered. "Don't let him mess with your head. I'm here for you. Dae is here. Gareth, the team, we all care about you so much."

Vidar hid his smirk into Boyd's soft wet hair. "Thank you, baby."

"Come over tonight?" He asked as he pulled back and Vidar knew in that second their Daddy/boy play was over, and he liked it. He liked it a lot. Daddy/boy he could do for a short time. But this? This conversation, he wanted to be Boyd and Vidar.

Kissing his forehead, Vidar agreed. "I'll text you when I'm done." Boyd smiled tiredly and Vidar couldn't resist those lips.

Chapter Fifteen

Running late...

His dad would kill him if he was late. Glancing at the clock, he pressed his foot a little firmer on the pedal. He had stopped off at his flat to change into *appropriate* clothes as his dad always said, and had to pull the Lamborghini out of storage. He hated the car. It was beautiful, but it was too flashy for him. However, his dad demanded he be picked up *in style.*

Vidar hadn't stopped sweating. The ease he felt after the shower he'd shared with Boyd didn't last long. His knees were scrunched up to the steering wheel, his lower back hurt in the too low bucket seats, and his necktie was choking him. Fortunately, it wasn't a long drive to the other side of The Thames but the mere thought of spending even an hour with his dad made his stomach clench.

Pulling up to the hotel's valet parking, he tossed the keys to the kid, accepted the ticket, and handed him some money.

"Won't be long," he said.

The valet acknowledged and Vidar entered the hotel. His father would not reply to an *I'm here* text. He wanted to flaunt who he was and claim happy family when all Vidar wanted was to grab some fish from the chippy and head home to Boyd. Home. Boyd had slept at his place, in his bed, exactly once and he was already calling it home with Boyd. Vidar rolled his eyes easing his heart and mind to get on the same page as he walked up to the reception counter.

"Welcome in, how can I help?" She greeted him with an appreciative once over.

"I'm Oskar Jørgensen's son. We have a dinner reservation. Could you call his room and let him know I'm here, please?" He asked.

"Certainly, Mr. Jørgensen, one moment." She picked up the desk phone and made the call. "He'll be right down." She let him know.

"Thank you," Vidar tapped the top of the counter absentmindedly and turned away to the lobby.

"Excuse me," Vidar looked over at a man approaching him. "Did you say Oskar Jørgensen? Like the MidFielder for ManU?"

Vidar took a silent breath. He was used to that. It was what his father wanted. He wouldn't be surprised if his father had set it all up. "Yes, my father."

"Oh wow, I'm a big fan," the man gushed. "My dad took me to the games as a kid. Your dad signed my jersey."

"He'll be down shortly. I'm sure he'd love to see you again," Vidar offered.

"How amazing it must have been for you! Growing up on the pitch, watching your dad."

Forcing a smile, Vidar held in his grimace. Though his father's anger on the pitch was well documented, anytime they would go out as a family, he would threaten Vidar to smile and not embarrass him. And it was Vidar's job to get info and pass it along to his father to look like he actually cared about his fans.

"What game was it that he signed your jersey?" Vidar asked, hating himself as he did.

"Oh god, years ago obviously. But it was against Chelsea."

"Always a fun game." *What the fuck am I doing?* He wondered.

"I'll say."

"There's my boy!" Vidar flinched and forced a smile when he turned to see his father hurrying to him. His dad threw his arms around him.

"Far, god kveld," he greeted him in Norwegian. Then, he continued telling him the man watching them, was a fan and he had signed his jersey at a Chelsea game a while ago. Once he'd conveyed the important details, he switched to English as he'd done before many many times. "Dad, this is a fan of yours."

"Jim Forster, Mr. Jørgensen. Big fan!" the man proclaimed as he took Oskar's outstretched hand.

"Oh, how nice," Oskar said with a genuine smile. "But, I remember you, don't I? Didn't I sign something for you once? A... a jersey?"

Vidar had to give his dad credit. He could bullshit with the best of them.

"Oh my god, you remember me?" The man gushed.

"Of course I do! I wouldn't be where I am without my fans. I try to remember all of you! You were much younger then," he teased. "But then, so was I."

"I can't believe it! Wow! Could I get a picture?" The man asked.

"Of course," his father exclaimed and opened his arm to him. The man hurriedly saddled up to him and snapped a selfie.

"Thank you so much!"

"Anytime!" His father watched the man leave and turned to Vidar. Speaking in Norwegian, he continued. "Haven't lost your touch, boy. Always could count on you."

"Yeah, of course. Ready? Reservations are in twenty."

"Good," his father stepped up beside him and slung his arm around Vidar's shoulders causing Vi to have to duck. His father was nearly eight inches shorter than he was and the angle was awkward. But the awkwardness increased when they walked out of the hotel to get the Lambo from the valet. Vidar saw a dozen or so paparazzi being held back by hotel security. They were shouting at his dad calling for a picture or his attention. The more racket they made; the more people took notice. His father laughed excitedly and waved to the crowd. It helped he wore Manchester United colors on his tie and pocket square. Vidar's stomach dropped.

"Did you do this?" He asked in Norwegian.

"Must stay relevant. Have I taught you nothing? Now, smile and wave, Vidar."

Those words snapped in his mind, and he obeyed without thinking. When his brain finally caught up, he hated himself.

"We'll miss the reservation," Vidar reminded him.

"Get to the valet. Bring the car around while I greet my fans."

"Yes sir," he immediately replied and cringed internally as soon as he turned away. He felt twelve again, not three times that age. He headed to the valet station and spoke to the kid who fortunately looked confused as to who the people worshiped. Without waiting too long, Vidar breathed a sigh of relief when his car was brought around.

The Lambo got as much love as his father. ManU red with gold trim, it was his father's, purchased for him many years ago. Vidar never drove it. He'd let Gareth and Dae-Hyun drive it once but as pretty as it was, a Lambo was not for men over six-foot-five.

"Far," he called to his father as he stood at the raised door of the driver's side and rested his hand on the roof. The clock on the valet's station showed he had seven minutes to get to the restaurant across the river and at that time of evening, it could take anywhere from ten minutes to two hours. The thought of spending two hours cooped up in the Lambo with his father was enough for him to break out in hives and hyperventilate.

His father finally seemed to sense the urgency and wrapped up the impromptu meet 'n' greet and headed to the car. But of course, he had to take pictures in front with the Lambo. Vidar shook his head and slipped into the seat. He had been told by more than one of his dad's old teammates they didn't appreciate the image Oskar gave to the team. But there was nothing Vidar could do.

Grabbing his phone, his thumb hovered over the old captain of the team's name. They texted often even not talking of his father, and he wanted so badly to talk to him. Boyd was right, the captain was more like a father to him than Oskar had ever been. He clicked on the text icon and typed out a short message.

Vidar: He's here. Paps everywhere. Pretty sure he called them. Sorry for not stopping him. I know the team doesn't need this.

Sending before his dad got in the passenger side, he didn't expect to get a reply that evening. Cap was a busy man. Sighing, his dad settled in the seat next to him.

"Hello, old girl, did you miss me?" He asked the car as he caressed the leather. Vidar put the vehicle in gear and pulled away from the curb. "Well, that was exciting," his dad said.

"*Far,* you know the team doesn't like it when you do that. I know you like the attention, but the reputation of the club is more important, don't you think?" Vidar offered.

"Oh piss off, I helped build that team. They sucked until I got there."

Vidar bit back the reproach on the tip of his tongue as his phone buzzed in his pocket. "I'm just thinking about—"

"Today went great, by the way, thanks for asking," his dad said, and Vidar knew that tone. He was in trouble. Gripping the steering wheel, the leather creaked under the pressure. He was a grown ass man; he shouldn't still get cold sweats at his dad's tone of voice.

"I'm glad. What happened?"

Oskar began explaining what the practice run through for the award ceremony was like. He chattered while Vidar tuned him out. He honestly wanted to be anywhere but where he was. Finally, they reached the restaurant, a full ten minutes late. He prayed to whatever deity was listening that they had held their reservation. He'd never hear the end of it if they didn't. Following his father into the restaurant after handing the keys to the valet, he pulled out his phone as it buzzed again. He had two texts waiting for him.

Cap: I got the notification earlier. I hoped he hadn't bothered you. Where are you? Please don't tell me you're going out with him.

Vidar swallowed. Cap was his code for the captain of ManU. Even though he was the manager, he'd always be the captain to him. And in case his father saw his phone, it was easy to explain away who "Cap" was without telling him. Namely, his old commander in the military and not the man who protected him as best he could when he was a boy.

Vidar: I had no choice, you know that.

He clicked to the other text chain and a soft smile instantly lifted his lips.

Boyd: Thinking about you and hoping everything is going okay, boyfriend. *winky face emoji* I was getting dressed to dance and you came to my mind.

Vidar licked his lips as memories of Boyd on that pole came flooding back. Not the best time to pop a boner, but he texted back.

Vidar: Needed that, baby, thank you. It's going to be a long evening.

The Captain's text dropped down in his notifications as he sent the message to Boyd.

Cap: I know. I'm sorry, Vi. Can I help?

Vidar: Thanks, I'm good, though. My boyfriend is on call if I need an exit.

His stomach dropped as soon as he reread his text. He hadn't been thinking as he typed. He never understood the need for a recall button until that moment.

Boyd's text popped down.

Boyd: I'm at my flat. Still want to come over afterward?

Vidar: Yes, I just outed myself to my father's captain. I was texting him warning about dad's antics and I mentioned my boyfriend. I'm freaking out.

Boyd: Baby, it's okay. Whatever fallout happens, I'm with you.

Vidar: Promise?

Boyd: I do. *two men kissing emoji*

Boyd: Sorry, got ahead of myself *winking emoji*

Vidar grinned. Boyd always knew how to break the tension.

"Is that Lynette?" His father asked. Vidar looked up, his brow furrowing, and he only *just* stopped himself from asking "who?" and smiled, nodded, and sat at the table the host indicated. "I like her, son." His father promptly poured a glass of gin he had requested be on ice for when they got there. His father loved gin but was oddly allergic to juniper, so the alcohol affected him quickly.

His phone buzzed and Vidar looked down, swallowing hard when he saw the name,

Cap: One question... is he a ManU fan? If not, you do NOT have my blessing, ha!

Vidar's chest lightened and tears nearly instantly filled his eyes. He stopped them quickly and clicked over to Boyd's text chain.

Vidar: Before I say yes to your proposal *winky emoji* Are you a ManU fan?

Boyd: If that's all it takes to get you, I'll deck my place out in red and gold. I'm sure my grandfather would be rolling over in his grave if he saw it… he was a Chelsea fan…

Vidar: Eh, Chelsea is better than Liverpool.

Boyd: Everyone hatin' on Liverpool… but that's okay. I'm afraid I'll lose you when I admit this, but I'm pretty neutral on football. Never got into it.

Vidar: I can change that… I have creative ways of persuasion.

Boyd: Yes please!

He clicked over to the captain's text chain.

Vidar: Indifferent. But at least not a Liverpool fan.

Cap: God forbid! Bring him to the box next Saturday. I'll send you two tix. Love to meet him!

Vidar let that text fill him with warmth until his father spoke up.

"All right all right, tell the little minx if she wanted to monopolize your time, she should have come. Though I'm sure you made sure she did before you left, right?"

An image of Boyd on his knees covered in cum flashed in his mind and he grinned. "Oh yes," he answered.

"My boy," the pride in his father's voice was hard to miss as he poured another glass of gin. Vidar wasn't sure how much he had already drunk but the bottle was already a fourth gone. "Have you told your mother about her?"

"No," Vidar answered and sent Cap an affirmative text back before putting his phone upside down the table. "I haven't told anyone outside of the team or my friends. It's still somewhat new."

"Six months is new?" He tossed back another shot and poured another. "Hell, your generation is so complicated. I'd met your mother and knocked her up with you within three months."

He tossed back the shot.

"And look how that turned out," Vidar snipped and held his father's murderous gaze refusing to revert to that little boy again. His father hated being reminded of his failed relationship as it was a low time in the press for him. He hadn't even been married to Vidar's mother. But the failed *perfect family* image, the bad boy turned family man, was splashed all over the tabloids.

"Look," he said when Vidar didn't apologize. "I'm not saying your mother and I were the pinnacle of relationships but six months with a woman like that and she gets bored. You've got to nail her down quick or someone else will. Knock her up. Force her to stay." He tossed back another glass.

Vidar looked around at the patrons nearby catching the surprised and some disgusted looks they sent his way as they overheard his father's words.

"Far," he started and continued in Norwegian. "Perhaps we should stick to our language if you're going out be vulgar."

"Oh, fuck 'em, who cares what a few people think," he stated in English as he tossed the next shot back.

Fortunately they were saved by the waitress walking over. "Good evening, gentlemen," she said, setting a basket of bread on the table. "I'm Lily, what can I get started for you?"

"Aren't you just the prettiest little thing," his father said.

As his father flirted with the woman twenty-five years his junior, and ordered nearly £1000 worth of food, appetizers, and another bottle of gin, Vidar stared. Really stared at him trying to see any similarity between them. He had his father's eyes and facial features, but his height and build came from his mother's side because, other than his eyes and cheekbones, he couldn't see much similarity between them. They couldn't be more different in personality and to Vi, it was a chore to be out with him. He didn't love his father; he didn't even like him. Any need to be with him was out of a sense of duty because he shared DNA with the man. But at that moment, he wanted to be anywhere but there.

His phone buzzed on the table and as his father was distracted by the waitress, Vidar checked the text. It was from Boyd. It was a picture message and Vidar nearly choked. The dark background with sensual red lighting was one he remembered vividly. Then, looking closer, he could just see Boyd's outline with more detail on his face, right shoulder, and part of his chest. He was shirtless, but Vidar could make out the black leather harness wrapped around his left pec and right shoulder. His head was thrown back exposing the tantalizing bit of neck and jaw and his full, sinful lips were parted on a soft gasp. He wore heavy, almost Egyptian looking eyeliner and the glitter was back. Vidar liked that glitter... Boyd's right arm was raised to hold the dance pole behind him. The image would live rent-free in Vidar's head for the rest of his life.

"Víðarr," he heard his father call his traditional pronunciation and shook himself from his thoughts, his eyes wide. Oskar and the waitress were looking at him expectantly and for the first time in twenty years in front of his father, Vidar felt his cheeks flame red as a blush colored his cheeks.

"Sorry, ehum..."

"What are you looking at?" His father demanded and ripped his phone out of his hands.

"Far, no!" Vidar tried but it was too late. His father stared at the picture. Time stood still for Vidar as he stared in horror at his father. Oskar's face slowly morphed from confusion, to understanding, to disgust, to anger, and then his hard eyes looked

up at Vidar.

"What the fuck is this?" His father roared. "Who the fuck is this?"

"*Far,* I—"

"Are you looking at gay porn?" His father demanded.

"No, no that's not—"

"Then what the fuck is this?" He shouted.

A man in a suit arrived at the table. "Sir, I need you to lower your voice."

"Get the fuck out of my face," his father screamed and pushed the man away. "Who is this?" He demanded of Vidar.

Every fear, every worry, every pain, every thought of his father's disapproval melted away as he remembered Boyd's words; *I'm here. Whatever fallout happens, I'm with you. I want you so much. I've been yours since the first moment I saw you.*

And all his anxiety melted away. "That is Lynette or, as I know *him,* Boyd. My *boyfriend.*"

It was dead silent for a split second before his father lunged for him. "You son of a bitch! You know what I told you I'd do to you if you were a queer! I'll fucking kill you!"

He got one hit in, and Vidar's cheek throbbed from the punch, but he was able to fend his father off with ease. Other patrons and staff leapt to his aid and held Oskar back as Vidar stood staring at the man he had feared for thirty-six years spew his hatred. But Vidar miraculously didn't hear any of it.

He waited until his father's mouth stopped moving, then he spoke. "Are you done?"

Oskar wasn't done, so Vidar waited. Finally, it looked like he lost steam and Vidar spoke again. "Oskar Jørgensen, ladies and gentlemen. My father as I'm sure you all heard, the bigot, homophobe, and drunk. Yes, I'm gay and there's nothing you can do about it. You can rage, beat me, disown me, hate me, hell even kill me or try because you won't be able to, but you can't change the fact that *your son* is gay. And you know what? I'm proud of it. I've lived with your hatred and bigotry so long you know what I say? Fuck you, there is nothing wrong with me. I have the love of the most amazing man who I love more than life.

"For years, I lived in denial dating women because it's what *you* wanted. I'm done trying to be good enough for you. I'm done doing what *you* want. If you can't accept this part of me, you are not my father, and I am not your son. I wish you would get the help you so desperately need. And I wish you well. But don't call me. Don't try to see me. And don't even try to contact me. I have a family. Yes, it's a found family, but I have brothers, a man I look up to and respect as a father, and I have people who actually care about me, and accept me. And guess what? That means you're not needed.

"I don't need your approval. I don't need your love and I'm sick and tired of trying to do everything you want and chasing the nonexistent carrot you dangle of *happy family*. I'm gay, Dad. Maybe I was born this way, maybe I was looking for a man's love, either way, you can blame yourself. So thanks, because of you, I get to spend the rest of my life with the *man* I love. And I don't give a damn what you think."

The applause surprised him, and Vidar flinched only to see the entire restaurant watching and cheering him on. Police officers approached and Vidar watched his father be handcuffed and hauled out of the dining room as he still spouted his vile hatred. The manager rushed over to him.

"I'm so sorry about this," Vidar said seeing the mess of the table and chairs and the disturbance they caused. "I'll pay for any damage."

"No damage," the manager answered. "Are you all right?"

"Thank you. You know, I think so," Vidar replied.

"You were so brave," a young mother said as her kid bounced in his seat waving at him. Vidar smiled and waved back.

"It sounds like it's been a long time coming," the manager said.

"That was awesome," a young man with black nail polish and the tips of his black hair dyed green rushed over. "You're, like, my hero."

Vidar smiled at the kid. "Thanks, but I'm not much of a hero."

"I disagree," another man spoke up from the bar. He eyed Vidar up and down. "Can I get you a drink?"

"Boyfriend, sorry," he thanked him. The man gave an *ah* and raised his glass to him in toast.

"Can I get you anything?" The manager asked.

"I think I'll just pay for dad's drinks and leave, if that's okay. I'll give you my info if there's anything else I need to pay for, but there's someone I need to see."

"Of course, let me get you some pasta and dessert to take with you, on the house," the manager offered.

"Oh, you really don't have to do that. We've caused enough problems for you already."

"It's no trouble," the manager said. "And it's my pleasure. Won't be two ticks."

"Thank you," Vidar called after the manager as he retreated into the kitchen.

Taking a breath, he turned when he heard the tinkling of

broken glass. A couple of the waiters were cleaning up what looked like their broken water glasses and the fallen bottle of gin.

"Can I help?" He offered.

"We have the tools, not to worry, sir," the boy with black nails and green hair said. "You've been through enough." He tossed his head back moving his skater-boy bangs.

Feeling out of place, he made his way to the front to wait for the manager. People clapped him on the shoulder and congratulated him as he passed. He knew everything would come crashing down on him soon enough, but he pulled out his phone and texted the details to Cap, who instantly called him.

"What the fuck?" He demanded by way of greeting.

"Yeah," Vidar breathed.

"Where are you? Let me pick you up," he offered.

"Thanks, Cap, but I'm good. I'm going to Boyd's."

"Boyd... that's the boyfriend?" There was no animosity or judgement in Cap's voice.

"Yeah," he answered.

"Okay, keep me posted, Vi. I'm here if you need to talk."

A lump formed in Vidar's throat. "Thank you." He wasn't accepted by his father, hated even, but like Boyd said, someone can fill their part of his heart to overflowing, and it helped soothe the burning gaping hole in his chest left by the man who fathered him. He hung up with Cap when he saw the manager come up to him, a takeaway bag in his hand.

"I threw some fresh bread in there too," he said.

"Thank you, I appreciate it."

"You have a good evening, now, understand?" The manager ordered.

Vidar nodded and pulled out his wallet. Handing him a

couple hundred-pound notes, he indicated the two busboys still cleaning the mess. "Please split this between them and our waitress, Lily I think."

"Very generous, thank you, sir, I'll make sure they get it."

"Thank you." He headed to the door hearing some clapping behind him, he turned and thanked everyone with a nod before he left the restaurant.

"Mr. Jørgensen?" A police officer asked.

"Not anymore," he answered. He was sure his father had disowned him, but he'd keep the name in honor of his grandfather who helped raise him. "But yes?"

"We need a statement from you, sir. Could you come to the station with us?" The officer asked.

"Can I come in tomorrow?" He asked. "My head's all over the place and I really need to see my boyfriend."

"Take a moment to write down as much as you can remember, while it's still fresh," the officer encouraged.

"Doubt it will stale anytime soon," Vidar answered. "But thank you. I'll be there by 0900 tomorrow."

"Here's my card. As for me at the front desk," the officer handed him the small business card and turned away. Before Vidar got to the car the valet pulled up for him, the officer turned back. "Don't worry, sir, we're going to keep him for 72 hours. You're safe."

Vidar chuckled. He had no doubt.

Chapter Sixteen

Boyd turned off the tap and opened the glass door of the shower when he heard his flat buzzer sound. Brow furrowed, he wrapped the towel around his waist and hurried to the intercom.

"Yes?" He answered.

"It's me," he recognized Vidar's voice.

"Vi?" He glanced at the clock. "You're early... really early, everything okay?"

"A lot of stuff happened," Vidar answered.

Oh god, Boyd thought. "Come up." He buzzed him in and rushed to his bedroom. Drying off as fast as he could, he pulled on his calf length yoga pants and threw on an old crop top t-shirt. Not exactly how he wanted to answer the door, but it was all he had time for. "Hey LOVE," he called to his AI.

"Yes, baby?" The AI asked.

"Turn on my 80s music and turn it down to level seven."

"Okay. Turning on 80s playlist at level seven."

"Thanks," he said and just as George Michael began singing softly in the background, Vidar knocked on the door. He rushed to the door and swung it open. "Oh, Vi?" He breathed softly. If the glaring red blotch on his cheek wasn't enough for him to know something happened, the look in his eye said plenty. "What happened?"

Vidar swallowed hard and held up the takeaway bag. "I brought dinner."

"Come in, talk to me."

Vidar did and Boyd watched him closely. It looked like he was... not depressed exactly, as his shoulders were up and not hunched, but he definitely looked like he needed to talk. But he didn't. And as he started pulling out the delicious smelling pasta dishes, Boyd hurried to the cabinet and grabbed a couple plates and a red wine bottle he kept for when he ate carbs. He opened the bottle and peeked at the Fettuccine Alfredo and Penne Arrabbiata. His mouth watered.

They served themselves and sat at the small kitchen bistro table, eating the first few bites in silence. Boyd couldn't stand the silence any longer, even Ms. Bonnie Tyler singing about a hero wasn't enough to break the tension.

"Was this the place you took your dad tonight?" He asked. Vidar nodded. "It's good," Boyd complimented. "Can you tell me what happened?"

Vidar let out the saddest, yet most liberating sound Boyd had ever heard.

"I was already nervous. He had tipped off the paparazzi and they were waiting for us at the hotel. But when we were at the restaurant, I was texting you and Cap, and Dad was getting drunk. I should have known he was going to do it, but I didn't think he'd actually grab my phone out of my hands and look at what I was doing. He saw your picture."

Boyd closed his eyes. *Shit.* He had taken the picture just before he worked out, hoping it would make Vidar smile and want to come over afterward but to know Oskar had seen the picture... *I'm going to be sick.*

"Vi, I'm so sorry," he looked up at him.

Vidar's head snapped up to look at him. "Sorry?"

"I didn't mean for anything like that to happen. Please believe me."

Vidar stared for a long moment, then reached over the table, palm up, silently asking for Boyd's hand. Boyd slipped his fingers through Vidar's and as soon as they closed over each other's, Vidar pulled him to his lap.

"You gave me the power and desire to be true to myself." He kissed his hair and Boyd nearly purred. "I came out to him. It's probably all over the internet by now. I bet someone filmed it. But he hit me once and then I realized how puny he was. How insignificant. And how much he ran my life even now. Dae mentioned that at lunch, and he was right. I was done playing the perfect son for an imperfect father. He never loved me. I was an inconvenience, something he used to keep my mother around because he liked the image we three projected. The perfect family. He could exploit it. Make himself look better. He got arrested and the people applauded me. Me! The manager gave me the food and one guy offered to buy me a drink. He was interested." Boyd clutched him closer, and Vidar chuckled. "I told him I had a boyfriend." Boyd was immensely satisfied with that and might have preened a bit. "But people were cheering for me because I broke free of him because of you. I knew you were here, and I wanted to be with you. I...need to tell you something," he pulled back and Boyd took the cue to lean away and lock eyes with him. Vidar took a breath but didn't look like he was debating it. "Boyd, I love you."

Boyd's breath caught. He hadn't heard those words since his family died and never from a man he wanted as a lover.

"You don't have to say it back, but you need to know. Over these last few months, you've grown so dear to me. I want to make you happy. I want to make you smile. I love your intelligence, your abilities, you are a fighter and to an old soldier like me that's a big turn on. But you need to know how precious you are to me. You've awakened a part of me I kept buried for over twenty years and gave me a safe place to be who I truly am. When my dad was spewing his hate and even when people were congratulating me, all I wanted was to be with you. I couldn't leave that place fast enough. You are home for me, and I love you so much."

Boyd's vision swam as he gazed up at Vidar's handsome face. The square jaw covered in a 5 o'clock shadow, the aquiline nose, the lips equally full top and bottom, the high cheekbones, pronounced forehead, and startling blue eyes, his magnificent body straining the white button up shirt's seams. And he was his. Boyd grinned and shook his head at the same time.

"I don't know what love it. I don't know how it feels," he cupped his jaw and stared deeply into those aquamarine eyes. "Show me? Make *love* to me. I know I care about you so much, but if you show me, I'll be able to put a name to what I feel."

Vidar leaned into his touch. "I would love nothing more. But you'll have to guide me on some things. I don't want to hurt you and I don't know what I'm doing."

Boyd smiled softly at his open honesty. "It would be my pleasure."

Without another word, or caring about the dishes, Boyd got up from Vidar's lap and, keeping their hands locked, he walked them to his bedroom. The salt lamp was the only light and his eyes glanced around the room. He was oddly nervous. He was never nervous in bed, usually, but his palms grew sweaty, and his legs trembled slightly. Not from fear, though, Boyd had seen Vidar's size and he was certain it would wreck him in the best possible way. He was nervous because... he didn't know... was he excited? Definitely.

Vidar's hand squeezed his and Boyd looked up at him as he wrapped his arms around him like a warm cocoon.

"I'm nervous. I don't want to hurt you," Vidar said.

"I'm nervous too. Excitedly so. And yes, it might hurt, you are the biggest I've ever taken, but I cannot wait to feel you inside me. We'll go slow at first. I'll tell you how I feel."

"Promise?"

"Promise."

Vidar nodded. "One other thing?"

"Name it."

"I... liked the Daddy/boy play earlier, but I want it to be just us right now."

Boyd smiled and squeezed the back of Vidar's neck. "Me too. I'm not one to want to live in that dynamic, more power to those who do, I know some who love it 24/7 but that's not me. We can be kinky whenever you want, but I agree. Tonight is for us.

Vidar and Boyd."

"What's your middle name? I don't even know it." Vidar blurted and Boyd recognized it as a stall tactic. He indulged.

"I was named after my grandfather. Boyd Vincent Falstaff."

"Vincent..." Vidar nodded. "I like it."

"And yours? Let me guess it's some unpronounceable Norwegian name?"

Vidar chuckled. "My mother is Swedish, so she named me." Boyd waited. "Ingemar."

"Ingemar?" Boyd questioned. Vidar nodded. "What does it mean?"

"Of the sea. Ing is a Norse god of fertility and peace. Ingemar was his son."

Boyd stared, then giggled. When Vidar questioned him with a beautiful smile, he shook his head. "I was just thinking about when your father said we'd make beautiful babies."

Vidar chuckled. "Want to practice?" He winked and Boyd burst out laughing. Without thought, he wrapped his arms around Vidar's neck and jumped. Vidar caught him under his ass and held him close as Boyd locked their lips together. Boyd sipped on his lover's lips and taste until his head spun. All his blood was rushing south, and his yoga pants were getting too tight.

When he came up for air, he spoke, his lips dancing with Vidar's. "I want you to make love to me tonight, but I want you to fuck me into the mattress tomorrow." Vidar's kisses faltered and Boyd leaned back slightly to see Vidar's eyes, black pupils dilated, nearly eclipsing the blue irises. "You good with that, Thor?"

Nodding quickly, he pulled Boyd back to him. "Yeah, baby," he said between kisses. "I'm good with that."

Boyd felt Vidar set his knee on the mattress and soon the

world tilted as Vidar laid them down. He didn't worry about the feeling of falling. He knew beyond a shadow of doubt Vidar would catch him, as he would catch Vidar. Their bodies lined and fit together perfectly. Groaning as their hard lengths rubbed behind the confines of their clothing. Boyd pushed on Vidar chest and the larger man pulled back.

"You're wearing too many clothes." His fingers shook. That time, he knew it was from adrenaline and excitement as he unbuttoned Vidar's white shirt. The taut skin being revealed button by button, proved too much for Boyd's self-control. He leaned up and dived in, licking and sucking love bites into Vidar's skin. His lover's hands dug under his crop top and tugged. Boyd's and Vidar's shirts landed in a pile together and Boyd rolled them over. Straddling Vidar's hips, he touched and caressed and smoothed his hands over the tanned skin.

"Your body is a work of art." The vulnerability in Vidar's eyes caused a lump to form in Boyd's throat. He could see the love, feel it in his hands, and taste it in his mouth. He finally understood the line from the old Disney movie, *so this is love?*

Boyd's hands caressed Vidar's chest, thumbs glancing off his nipples. His lover hissed and Boyd smiled. "Like that?" Vidar nodded and Boyd leaned down, taking one taut bud into his mouth. Vidar squeaked, then let out the sexiest moan Boyd had ever heard.

Licking and sucking the bud to a tight point, Boyd dragged his tongue across the hairless chest and laved attention on the other. Vidar squirmed beneath him. From his seated position, Boyd felt Vidar's cock twitch and undulated his hips a little.

"Stop stop," Vidar panted. "Gonna come. Too close."

Boyd grinned but stopped and pulled off the nipple with a

pop and looked up at his lover's face. His chest and neck were flushed, and he had his arm flung over his eyes.

After a beat, he spoke low, not moving his arm. "That was embarrassing."

Boyd giggled. "Happens to the best, baby."

Another beat and Vidar finally looked up at him. They were silent for a long time before Vidar caressed Boyd's sides and ogled his naked torso. His yoga pants did nothing to hide his erection, straining to get loose. Vidar's fingers slipped under the waistband and tugged. Boyd's ass and cock were revealed and cooler air caressed his heated skin.

"You are so beautiful," Vidar breathed, his gaze hot and soon his eyes zeroed in on Boyd's length. "I've never touched another man's dick before."

"Good, and you're not going to touch anyone else's but mine, understand?"

Vidar grinned. "Yes, baby. And the same goes for you, you know. I don't share well."

"Join the club."

With that, Vidar pushed up and turned them back over. Boyd locked his ankles around Vidar's waist as he leaned down and devoured his mouth. No other words were exchanged as Vidar pulled back and tugged Boyd's yoga pants off. The sound of his belt clanging and the zipper being lowered was lewd and loud in the stillness, but Boyd loved every second. He stared, his eyes heavy lidded as he took in Vidar's glorious body, muscled thighs, tight abs, tan skin, and thick cock bobbing between his legs. As Boyd stared at the monster, Vidar's hand stroked it.

"Please," Boyd whispered and reached for him, licking his lips.

"I don't want to hurt you."

"You won't." That might have been a lie. Boyd was fairly certain Vidar could tear him in two, but he knew how much pleasure awaited them both. "Come to me."

Vidar let out a pained sigh as if he was waiting for those words. Crawling up Boyd's body, Vidar took time to kiss, lick, and suck every inch of him, except the part that throbbed so desperately. By the time Vidar reached his lips, Boyd was quivering and closer to orgasm than he had any right to be. The mood had shifted, and Boyd was certain Vidar felt it too. They were playful before, but as the reality loomed before them, they grew more serious.

"Show me what to do," Vidar said softly.

"Stretch me open," Boyd replied and reached for the lube he kept in his nightstand drawer.

"Condom?" Vidar asked and Boyd paused.

"I have the one I commandeered from your bathroom but..." he paused. "I'm clean. I've never done this without a condom... not willingly at least. I'd... I want to feel you and I don't want anything between us. Would that be all right with you?"

Vidar licked his lips and nodded. "I've never done this without one either," he confessed. "But I want to with you."

Boyd reached up and brought Vidar's lips closer to him. Kissing him, lube forgotten for the moment, he reveled in the press of their naked bodies. Vidar groaned and began to thrust his hips in short movements rubbing their aching shafts against each other. Boyd's orgasm came roaring back, and he broke the kiss so fast, his head spun. Panting, he pressed one hand to Vidar's chest.

"Too close," he laughed.

Panting, "me too," Vidar said.

Boyd shrugged. "Well, I know I'd recover quickly, but you're an old man, might be a one and done night for you." Boyd bit his lip teasingly.

"Oh you think so, do you?"

Boyd shrieked a giggle as Vidar tickled his sides. "Oh god, oh god, oh god!" he gasped. "Mercy!"

Vidar laughed and Boyd decided it was his favorite sound. "Old man, my arse," Vidar teased.

The short reprieve did the trick to calm them both down and as Boyd burrowed into his mattress looking over at Vidar who had moved to his side next to him, he pushed his fingers through the short hair on the side of Vidar's head.

"I've never had a guy stay over," he said softly. "Be here when I wake up?"

"I'm not going anywhere, baby," Vidar stated.

With that promise, Boyd handed him the bottle of lube and showed him how to prep him. When Vidar's thick finger penetrated him, he gasped and groaned in joy. It was too much and not enough all at once.

As Vidar scissored his fingers, he let out a breath. "You are so tight. I don't want to hurt you."

"You won't," Boyd answered on a gasp as Vidar's third finger curled and brushed against his prostate.

"How do you know? I'm... not exactly small. I don't want-"

Boyd stopped him by cupping his face. "Because I trust you. Please, I need you. I want you inside me," Boyd begged.

They stared at each other for a long moment before Vidar removed his fingers and moved to hover over him.

Vidar kissed him, plundering his mouth with his tongue. Head swimming in ecstasy, Boyd took Vidar's cock and guided it to his entrance. "Make love to me."

With a whimper, Vidar's head buried into Boyd's neck, he notched the head of his shaft against Boyd's entrance and pushed in slowly. Boyd clawed at his massive back as he felt the tip of Vidar's cock breach his hole. Boyd felt the sting as Vidar's inexperienced fumbling pushed him deeper too quickly. Boyd breathed through the slight pinch and whispered "slower".

Vidar reared back and looked down at him. His pupils completely blown and sweat dripped down his forehead. "Did I hurt you?"

Boyd shook his head. "You're just bigger than I expected."

"I'm sorry," Vidar kissed his cheek first one then the other.

"Don't be," Boyd said. "I'm fine, promise. Just go a little slower. Let me adjust to you."

Vidar nodded vigorously. It was almost comedic how slowly he took things but inch by torturous inch, Vidar slid inside him, pulled out, then slid in a little more than before, and pulled out again.

He faltered when Boyd spasmed around him and grunted. But soon, he bottomed out and Boyd had never felt so full.

"Oh god, yes!" Boyd cried out, delirious with need.

Vidar panted into his neck and paused. "So tight."

"Don't stop, please. I'm okay now, don't stop!"

"I love you," Vidar said softly into his ear before he pulled out almost all the way and locking eyes with him, slid inside with one steady thrust.

They cried out in unison as Boyd felt him hit his prostate. And with the delicious feeling of Vidar's hard cock inside him, he shivered and spasmed, his orgasm just hovering. He'd never been so close so quickly.

"Vi, Vi, Vi," he panted as Vidar thrust into him again and again and again. "Oh, god! Yes!"

"Fuck," Vidar hissed.

The noises that filled the room were inhuman. Boyd whined grunted, groaned, and pleaded but after only a few minutes of wild, grunting pleasure, Vidar slowed. Slowed and pulled up. He stared down at Boyd, his face a mixture of fascination and awe. Vidar slowed to lazy movements as he took in Boyd's face. Boyd stared back, locking eyes with the blue ones he loved. He knew it in that moment.

Vidar's rocking still brushed over that sensitive spot inside him, but neither were in a hurry. They had all night.

"I love you," Vidar whispered again, and Boyd's breath caught at those words. "Thank you. Thank you for wanting me. This shy inexperienced, *formerly* straight guy with little to his name except a decent military career and a broken home life."

Boyd pushed up gently and Vidar went to his back willingly without breaking their connection. Boyd straddled him and placed his hands on Vidar's massive chest.

"One," he began. "You had one hell of a military career, and you should be damn proud of that. Two, the broken home life was your father's doing. You have friends, good friends who love you. A team who functions better *with* you. A beautiful companion who looks at you with her big, beautiful puppy dog eyes like you hung the sun and moon." Vidar smiled softly. "And you have me. I'm not much and I'm hardly special, but you have me. And... I love you more than anyone on this earth, Vidar Jørgensen. So, don't you ever think you have nothing. You have everything."

Vidar's breathing trembled and he sat up, wrapped his arm around Boyd's waist and cupped the back of his head. He thrust up into him and kissed him at the same time. Boyd cried out and surrendered to the bliss. He had never felt that way before. Had never known anyone could feel that way and as he rode his man, slowly, gently, staring down into his eyes, seeing the moment he let go, feeling him swell and spill inside him, Boyd threw his head back and his orgasm washed over him in warm loving waves. It wasn't his strongest orgasm, but in a way, it was his greatest.

Chapter Seventeen

Vidar woke slowly with a smile on his face. It was still pitch-black outside but the salt lamp on the nightstand cast the room in a soft orange glow. Memories flooded back to him, and he grinned as he took stock of how he felt. Sated. Languid. Happy. Peaceful. He took a breath and buried his nose into Boyd's hair as his head rested on Vidar's shoulder. The much younger man stirred, and his breathing deepened. Vidar watched in fascination as his eyes opened slowly and he looked up at him.

"Hey," Vidar breathed.

Boyd grinned and reached up to kiss him. "Hey." Vidar closed his eyes as Boyd's soft lips touched his. He lingered but the kiss stayed sweet. "How do you feel?" he asked, his voice just above a whisper.

Vidar beamed and squeezed him tighter. "Amazing." Boyd chuckled and kissed his shoulder. "How about you?" His hand slipped down to Boyd's ass and squeezed gently.

"I'll never lie to you, so I'll say, I'm sore, but I loved every second of it."

A twinge of guilt gnawed at Vidar, but Boyd crawled on top of him. "Don't," he said kissing his chest. "Yes, you're a big boy," he wiggled his eyebrows suggestively and Vidar chuckled. "But you were gentle... loving and I'll be fine by tonight."

"Tonight, huh?"

"I distinctively remember you promising to make love to me first then fucking me into the mattress the next time. I expect you to deliver on that promise, Jørgensen."

"And I will, but only when you're feeling all right. I can't hurt you."

"It would hurt me not to have you rail me good and hard. I want to feel you hitting my stomach, baby and with a cock as big as yours I want to be walking funny for a week."

Vidar chuckled, god, he'd never felt so free. He leaned back, tightened his arm around Boyd and threw his other forearm over his eyes surprised at the lump in his throat. Boyd must have sensed it because he went quiet and nuzzled his neck. Vidar swallowed around the lump, but it grew, and he hated the tears that gathered in the corners of his eyes. Boyd said nothing as he kissed Vidar's jaw, then the column of his neck and proceeded lower to the dip where his collarbone's gapped. He snaked his way down to Vidar's chest kissing and licking the smooth skin there. Vidar never liked hair on his chest. It was itchy, so he waxed whenever he needed it. As Boyd kissed him, his hands ran up and down his arms and sides. Vidar let the tears fall silently. He didn't know or understand why he was crying, but he couldn't stop. When he gasped for breath, Boyd moved up to him and blanketed him with his body.

"Shh shh," he soothed.

"I don't even know why I'm crying," Vidar sobbed. "I don't cry. Ever."

"Because you've always had to be strong, and you know you don't have to be with me. I love you."

Vidar sobbed and wrapped his arms around Boyd's body like a vice. "Say it again?"

Boyd's lips lifted on his neck, and he kissed just below his ear. "I love you."

Vidar's body relaxed and he gulped in air. Feeling his man in his arms, knowing and believing in his love, Vidar calmed. They were silent for a while just holding each other. Boyd's smaller frame fitting perfectly in his arms. The sun slowly rose, and they watched the sunrise together, not speaking. But with a deep breath, Vidar broke the spell and checked the time. He needed to give his statement to the police at 0900.

Rubbing Boyd's back, he kissed his hair and spoke low. "Can I use your shower?"

"Of course," he answered. "I'll get breakfast started. I'm hungry."

"Of course you are," he teased.

Boyd pretended to be offended as he sat up, straddling Vidar's hips and all Vidar could think of was staring up at him as he rode him in that position the night before. But his thoughts were interrupted by his phone buzzing. Boyd snatched it and shamelessly looked at it.

"Text from someone named Arianwen to you and Dae saying 1400 tomorrow works but doesn't say what," Boyd looked up at him and Vidar took his phone back.

"That's because it's a surprise," Vidar said.

"Ooh," he squirmed, and Vidar's blood rushed south hardening his morning wood even more. "I like surprises."

"I know," he grunted. "And don't think any amount of squirming on my todger will make me break my silence."

"You sure about that?" The look that entered Boyd's eyes should have worried him but Vidar just grinned as Boyd hurried down his body. Vidar groaned and threw his head back against the pillow when, without warning or hesitation, Boyd swallowed his cock, sucked, and licked, moaning like it was his favorite snack.

Seeing Boyd bob up and down taking as much of him as he could, Vidar plunged his fingers through his luscious brown hair. The soft, wet, heat encapsulating him in the best way possible.

"Jesus," he groaned. "Don't you have a gag reflex?"

"Mm, mm," he grunted around the thickness and Vidar clenched feeling the vibration around him. When Boyd slicked up his finger in the saliva dribbling down his length and circled Vidar's hole, pushing in ever so gently, Vidar cried out, *"å gud!"* and came, spilling down Boyd's convulsing throat.

The speed of his orgasm made him dizzy, and he panted, his body going boneless into the mattress. He felt Boyd's mouth pop off his cock and give the tip a kiss before he slipped up to Vidar. Lifting on his elbow, he looked down at him, smiling.

"Good?" He teased.

"Fishing for compliments?" Vidar panted.

Boyd beamed. "You are very sensitive. Would you ever consider bottoming?" He dragged his finger over Vidar's chest.

"It's not something I've thought of before, obviously," he said.

"Obviously."

"But," Vidar's hand stroked Boyd's bare leg. "I'd consider it with you."

"Oh good, I beat out Dae and Gare for your first," he winked.

Vidar laughed feeling freer than he'd ever felt before. Boyd was watching him, languidly caressing one of the scars on his chest.

"What did you say just then?" He asked.

"When?" Vidar questioned.

"When you came, sounded like *all good.*"

Vidar thought for a second. "Oh!" He remembered. *"Å gud,"* he said. Boyd nodded. "It basically means *oh god* in Norwegian."

"Norwegian is your native language, right?" Vidar nodded and Boyd continued. "What other languages do you speak?"

"Swedish, German, Dutch, and Urdu but it's only passible."

"Why those?"

"Scandinavian countries share a lot of base language with Germanic roots. My mother taught me Swedish, and I picked up German and Dutch in school. Urdu because I was stationed in Afghanistan for a while, and we picked up a lot from our translator."

"Is that where you got this?" Boyd asked stroking a knife wound scar.

"Yes, we were clearing a village and evacuating women and children when we came across a basement. Some Taliban soldiers were hiding out. Geoff, my commander and I fought them while the rest of the team got the women and children out of there.

Geoff's one hell of a soldier and a great commander and friend. When I heard him go down, I was distracted, and the soldier came at me. Cut me," he indicated the scar.

"What happened?"

"Geoff's all right. He's retired now living with his boyfriend. But Gareth put one between the soldier's eyes and it gave me enough time to get out of there."

"Did it hurt?"

"Not at first. You're running on adrenaline, but it stung a bit when sweat and sand got inside. Our medic Raj, patched me up after checking on the civies."

"And this one?" He touched a faded scar on his leg.

"Stray bullet during a fire fight. We were entrenched with enemy forces closing in from up high and the bullets were pinging off everything. Nearest as I could tell, it hit a rock and a part of it ricocheted to my leg. I didn't even know I was hurt until Geoff saw the blood."

"What about these?" Boyd touched a cluster of white scars on his side.

"Shrapnel. Suicide bomber blew himself up taking half a village with him. I was standing too close."

Boyd shivered and moved down to rest his head on his shoulder, still idly tracing the scars on his chest and arm. "When did you retire?"

"When they pulled out of Afghanistan. I had been in longer than some, but I couldn't stomach the idea of a desk job. So, I took my pension and my medals and hung up the uniform."

"My grandpa was in Lebanon during the Syrian crisis. He was a Royal Marine."

"They're tough old soldiers."

Boyd nodded sadly. "I have his medal. I used to hide it at the orphanage. They would come around and take whatever they thought would make them money. The nuns always turned a blind eye to what the boys had. It was nice of them, I guess. But when the state took over... the warden would take anything he wanted... including us."

Vidar wrapped his arm around him and squeezed. They lay there for a long while until his alarm went off. He had to get to the station and give his statement. Kissing Boyd's hair, he silenced the alarm.

"I have to go," he said. Boyd nodded into his chest and kissed the scar.

"I'll make you some breakfast," Boyd offered and leaned up to look at him. Vidar smiled, grasped the back of his head and brought him down to kiss him.

"Thank you," he mumbled against Boyd's lips.

Smiling, Boyd got out of bed and grabbed his yoga pants from the day before. Tugging them on, he tossed a kiss over his shoulder before leaving the room. Vidar took a moment. Staring up at the popcorned ceiling, he took in how he felt. He'd had sex... with a *man!* And he felt... good. It was almost as if he had a new lease on life. He was proud of who he was. Of whom he loved. And the strides he'd made the night before. Never had he been so happy. Sex with women was always a chore. Sex with Boyd... his cock twitched remembering. Grabbing his phone, he sent a text.

Vidar: You were right. It is amazing.

Getting up, he padded to the bathroom and turned on the shower. His phone dinged.

Gare: What?! Details!

Dae: Easy, babe, he'll tell us in his own time.

Vidar grinned.

Vidar: Never felt this way with a woman.

Gare: Damn you! Tell me everything!

Vidar: Boyd and I spent the night together. I came out to my dad. It's been a lot.

Dae: We know. There was a video. It's gone viral.

Vidar: Video?

Dae sent him a link. The video was of his confrontation with his father. The likes and comments were in the thousands. It was odd to see the conversation as an outsider. Parts he didn't even remember. The murderous look on his father's face was nearly comical. Against his better judgment he looked at the comments. Some were homophobic. Some were hurtful. But most of them were congratulatory, backing his decision, and putting his father down. His heart fell at that. No matter how bad his father was, he didn't want to cause him problems. Gare's text came next, and it gave him the excuse to get out of the video.

Gare: Dinner tonight? We need details.

Vidar: Have to see what the team needs but yes. That sounds great!

Boyd knocked on the bathroom door and Vidar turned to see him leaning against the frame. "Breakfast needs to wait."

"Oh? Why?"

"Because I saw this," Boyd showed the video.

"And?"

"And... I need to show you how much I love you and how hot you are." Boyd sauntered toward him and jumped into his arms. Vidar laughed as Boyd kissed him. Shower sex was never something on his list of things to try but the last two times he'd been in the shower with Boyd had been the best experiences of his life.

He smiled as he showed off the Lamborghini to Boyd. Then, kissed him goodbye, heading to Scotland Yard an hour later. He smiled as he handled his father's situation. He smiled as he headed to work. And his smile stayed in place until he reached the bunker and saw Gabe look up from his phone and share a looked with Nigel.

"Mate, what the hell? You slept with him and didn't tell us?" Gabe questioned.

His smile faded, only slightly. "Huh?"

Chapter Eighteen

Boyd turned on the tele after Vidar left and listened with one ear as he washed the dishes from dinner the night before and breakfast. But his mind was on his lover. His grin grew as he danced a little around his kitchen. He had slept with countless people but none of them made him feel giddy the next day. Getting dressed, he made the bed, taking a moment to sniff the pillow. He slammed his face into the pillowcase and inhaled.

God, he *loved* Vidar's scent. Reverently, he set Vidar's pillow back on the bed and caressed it. It would forever be known as *Vidar's.* Once dressed, he headed back to the kitchen to refill the coffee mug Vidar had given him earlier when he made the coffee, as Boyd cooked up some eggs. Next to the machine was a folded note with his name on it. Opening the paper, he recognized the Pig Pen Cipher and grinned. Quickly, he pulled up the cipher key on his phone and translated the note.

I L-O-V-E Y-O-U.

S-E-E Y-O-U A-T T-H-E O-F-F-I-C-E

V

Beaming, Boyd read the note and flipped the paper over. Writing a message on the back, he tucked it into his pocket, intent on slipping it into Vidar's pocket when he got to the office. Pouring the coffee in his insulated travel mug, Boyd caught the tail end of the news segment.

"An historic vote happened yesterday in Parliament as the Prison Reform Bill passed with just two signatures over what was needed. The bipartisan bill drew support and ire from both sides who fought it out on the floor of the Houses. One such argument made by the Tory MP, Lord Lyndon." The camera switched to who, Boyd assumed, was Lord Lyndon shouting in what Boyd called the *MP Voice.* A voice louder than usual with a distinct cadence.

"If this silly law passes, I ask you what's next? Mister Speaker, this trash should never have made it this far. Our duty is to the British people. We have a duty, a *duty* to protect them and this goes against that very foundation. Releasing non-violent offenders back onto the streets? I ask you, if they were non-violent, why were they charged, convicted, and sanctioned? Non-violent, that's a unique word, because I guarantee you all here today, that if we asked their victims, victims of armed robbery, molestation, pornography, drug trafficking, human trafficking, and yes Mr. Speaker, those fall under the Non-Violent Act, larceny, bribery, identity theft... I ask you, poll their victims. The young boy or girl who was molested by their creeper uncle, the parents of a sixteen-year-old drug victim who they just buried, the immigrant shop keeper who was held at knife point and told to empty the register. I tell you, if we ask them... would they say it was non-violent and agree to letting their attacker out? I say to you no. No. No. No. No. And it is our duty to listen to them and ensure this filth is never passed in this house."

The anchor came back on, but Boyd shook his head. For once, he actually agreed with a Tory.

Glancing back at the clock, he turned off the television and grabbed his shoes. Slipping on his coat, he headed to the door and opened it.

He froze.

"Hello малыш."

"Sasha?" Boyd tried to calm his racing heartbeat. "What... what are you doing here?" As casually as he could, Boyd placed his hand in his pocket and touched his phone.

"Aren't you going to let me in?" Sasha asked in a fake soft voice.

"Of course, yeah, sorry. You just surprised me."

Sasha walked in and it gave Boyd the split second he needed to unlock his phone and dial Vidar's number.

"I wouldn't be doing that, малыш." Boyd turned and inhaled sharply as he stared at the barrel of a gun pointed his way. He lifted his hands in the universal gesture.

"Sasha?"

"Put it down."

He did and set it on the entry table, face down as the call connected.

"Sasha, what are you doing here?" He asked hoping it was loud enough for Vidar to hear. Sasha just chuckled and walked to the entry table, grabbing the phone. Putting it on speaker, he spoke.

"I have your little one," he said. "He will not be hurt if you do exactly what I want." Sasha paused and Boyd waited to hear what Vidar said.

"What do you want?" Vidar asked.

"Hmm, good boy," Sasha cooed on the phone. "Now, I know of your little mission. I'm as curious as you as to what's in that vault. I wasn't given clear picture when I was recruited, and I need to know there is nothing... incriminating in there. You help me. I help you crack the code to Kyetti's accounts. I know your algorithm hasn't work on the majority of them."

"I don't need your help," Boyd spat.

"Ohoho, малыш you do. Your little sixth form hacking skills won't break through Kyetti's security.

"We can't trust you," Boyd heard Kiter say over the phone.

"No, but then the feeling is mutual. Now, you will stay out of my way as I take our little малыш with me to break into the vault. Once I have what I came for, Boyd will be freed. But you come after me, well," he pulled out his own phone and showed Boyd a picture.

"What?" Vidar's voice was strained as if he spoke through clenched teeth.

"Tell him, малыш."

"He has a picture of Hunter and Colton at practice," Boyd explained the picture Sasha was showing him.

"So you know. I have an arsenal of information and people working for me who would have no qualms in taking out two little boys. But I would prefer the next generation stay intact. So as soon as I have what I need, the stand down order will be given. Until then, know I have the most precious things in the palm of my hand. Make a move against me and they die. Try to stop me and Boyd will know just how rough I can be. He enjoyed it last time... I assure you; he will *not* enjoy it this time."

"After the dick I just took, I'd hardly feel yours," Boyd bit out.

"Want to see, малыш?" He sneered.

"Boyd, just do as he says," Vidar stated. "Sheila and Gareth want to see you again. So please. I'll tell Lynette you'll see her soon. Everything will be all right."

Boyd kept his face devoid of a reaction. He was going to get help. Dae and Gareth, they'd help Vidar. And it triggered his memory, Dae was in the vault area. And as for Lynette, Vidar was telling him to fake it and play along. Maybe even lure Sasha into a false sense of security.

"Okay," Boyd replied. "See you boys soon. Don't wait up." He threw in a joke as was his personality.

Sasha hung up the phone and looked at Boyd. His face softened as he tilted his head to one side.

"No hello kisses?" He asked.

"No," Boyd answered. "You threatened me and the people I love. You nearly killed Nigel!"

"You told me you didn't feel like you fit in with them. Now, barely a month later, you *love* them?"

"Yes. You were a mistake, Sasha."

"That's not what you called me that night. I've missed you, малыш and I never miss a onetime fuck."

"Are you trying to tell me you like me for more than a couple hours? Well, too bad, I didn't miss you. You nearly killed my friend!"

"He was no friend to you. You even said it. They never showed you meant something to them."

"I was wrong. And you hurt them for Kyetti. So whatever you're trying to do to me, stop. It won't work. I'll not join you. Let's just get this done so I can go."

Sasha's face hardened as he sneered. "Fine." He grabbed Boyd's arm tightly, but Boyd didn't cry out. He wouldn't give Sasha the satisfaction. Jack's face flashed in his mind. His strength and determination not to cry out. He would be just like that. He would not cry out.

Chapter Nineteen

Vidar paced. He should never have left him. He should never have left to go to Scotland Yard. He should have gone back to get him before going into work. He would never forgive himself if Sasha hurt him.

"Hey," Callum stepped into his path forcing him to stop pacing. "Boyd is smart. He'll be fine. And we need a plan."

"I shouldn't have left him. I shouldn't have—"

"Hey," Callum placed his hand on Vidar's shoulder. "You had to take care of your bad situation. Everyone understands that. Boyd doesn't blame you."

Gabe stepped up to him. "Don't you blame yourself. Trust me. I know how it feels to be hopeless and blame yourself for things out of your control." He glanced at his fiancé in his wheelchair. Nigel gave him a small smile. "But believe me when I say, it will make you feel better to make a plan."

"Take a breath," Callum ordered, and Vidar did. "Now, what do we know?"

"Sasha has Boyd," Vidar stated.

"And what does Sasha want with him?" Callum prompted.

"To break into the vault that we want."

"And why?"

"To get any incriminating information about himself," Vidar provided.

"And what can we do?"

Vidar swallowed, his mind clearer than a few minutes ago. "We have a friendly down there. We need to warn him and maybe get his help."

"Is he working today?"

Vidar thought for a moment. "No, but I'll call him."

"We have two of the best marksmen in the UK," Kiter stated. "Let's play to our strengths."

Vidar shook his head. "My hands are shaking too much, but Gareth can help." He refused to think of what Sasha could be doing to Boyd. He would save him. He would protect him. He had to. He loved him. Taking his phone, he dialed.

"Vi, dinner a go tonight?" Gare's voice came on the other end.

"Negative, Alice, we have a White Rose situation."

Gareth, Dae, and Vidar were part of Team Alice, the best covert recovery team in Afghanistan. Their team, based on Lewis Carroll's Alice in Wonderland, always used codes and phrases from the book. A White Rose situation meant trouble, mainly hostages.

There was a pause on the other end. Then, "what do you need?" Dae asked. Vidar breathed a little easier.

Boyd allowed Sasha to manhandle him into the van. There were five others inside, but they all wore ski masks. But what gave Boyd pause were the massive, military grade weapons they all carried.

"Shouldn't we tie his hands?" A central London accented voice asked.

"Think he can overpower us?" Sasha asked rhetorically.

"Looks can be deceiving," the same man said.

"I've been inside that body. I know what he is and isn't capable of," Sasha retorted.

"You sure it was your cock? Felt more like a finger," Boyd snipped. Sasha smirked and chuckled then looked at the man beside Boyd and gave a slight nod. Pain exploded across Boyd's face as his head whipped sideways and he tasted the metallic tang of blood.

"Oh, now you've done it. I was going to beg Vidar for mercy for you but now, the second he sees my busted lip and bruised face, is the second you die." Boyd licked his lips tenderly and winced as a headache began at his temples.

"If your man wants to see you alive again and not bleeding out of every orifice, he will do as he is told. Like you did, малыш. You know Daddy loved it when you did as I told you."

"You're not my Daddy. And I'm not your малыш. So shut up so we can make this whole ordeal easier on both of us," Boyd ordered.

"As you wish," Sasha conceded. They drove in silence for a while, but the sound of the road made Boyd antsy.

"How did you know about the mission?" He finally asked. Sasha raised an eyebrow.

"I thought we weren't talking."

Boyd shrugged. "I'm bored."

Sasha chuckled humorlessly. "We could do something that wouldn't be boring."

"Not interested. How did you know?"

Sasha stared at him for a long moment. Boyd couldn't honestly remember what it was about him he had found so attractive. Yes, he was rugged in a mountain man killer sort of way, but he much preferred the blonde Viking currently freaking out and probably blaming himself. *It's not your fault, Vi. Love you.*

"I have a contact who keeps me informed of your movements."

"Someone other than who you and Kyetti work for?" Boyd asked. Sasha shrugged. "How deep does the government corruption go?"

Sasha gave him a sardonic look. "Oh sweet малыш, do you honestly believe you and your band of merry men can stop all of it?"

"I'd just like to know what we're dealing with."

Sasha laughed. "You're naïve child."

"And you're an overconfident bully. So I guess we're even."

Sasha smirked but said nothing more. Boyd turned away from him and wished there were windows in the van. He hated tight spaces but surrounded by men with guns who could easily overpower him, had his anxiety sparking. He closed his eyes and swallowed the bile that rose. He would not get sick. He wouldn't give them the satisfaction of seeing him scared. But he couldn't seem to stop the memories of the warden. The fear, the pain, the humiliation. They suffocated him as he remembered his grimy hands on him. His breathing increased. He was on the verge of a panic attack.

I love you.

He gasped when the memory of Vidar saying he loved him, making love to him, holding him, kissing him, laughing with him. The feeling of his arms around him as they fell asleep that first night and every other time. The soft licks from Sheila as she whined and woke them up to go play. He remembered the blue of Vidar's eyes, the gold in his hair, the laughter on his face. He remembered the man he loved, and he held on to him. He trusted him. He'd have a plan. If Boyd couldn't get out of the situation alone, which his odds were increasingly low, he had no doubt Vidar would save him.

Sasha be damned. Boyd would be in Vidar's arms again very soon.

He didn't let the small voice inside his head take his hope but when the van entered the underground lot for MI6 agents with no pushback from the guard, Boyd's heart beat faster. He was unceremoniously dragged out of the van and one of the men behind him pressed the muzzle of a handgun into his lower back.

"Walk," he barked, and Boyd followed Sasha into the lifts. He kept his eyes sharp for any hint of Vidar and the team.

Nothing happened when they entered the lifts. Nothing happened as the lift moved down to SB9. Nothing happened when they walked out to the entry where Dae's team should have been.

Boyd's heart sank for a moment until, "You have entered an unauthorized space. All current exits are now sealed." He recognized Nigel's voice over the intercom just as the lights went off and the backup generator kicked on. They were bathed in muted red light and the mechanical clang of doors locking and latching resounded throughout the space. Boyd grinned as Sasha barked out orders in the harsh language of his native tongue. The gun pressing against his back vanished as the man raced to do whatever Sasha had said. But his freedom was short-lived as he felt Sasha's large hand grip his upper arm.

"These your friends?" He sneered.

"It took weeks for us to figure out a way of doing this and you just barge in with no recon and expect things to go your way? Boyd questioned. The look Sasha gave him was sickening. He moved and then pain registered in Boyd's body. He doubled over, the wind knocked out of him.

"You know what I promised to do to you if they interfered. Call them off. I'd hate to hurt your pretty face."

Boyd held in his victorious look. Sasha was nervous.

"Now move, малыш," Sasha said, then raised his voice as if speaking to whoever was on the intercom. "I will destroy him if you continue this. Back off now. Or you will be picking him up in pieces."

"Don't do it, boys!" Boyd shouted then groaned when Sasha punched his stomach again.

"If they want you alive, they will."

There was silence for a short time and Sasha pushed Boyd forward. Sasha's men were stationed at the exit doors and lift, ready and armed. Before Sasha got more than three steps, a shot rang out and one of the men at the lifts cried out and fell down.

Sasha whirled around to see the man beside the one on the floor, checking his buddy. Then, another shot and the man crouching cried out and fell to the ground.

"You, you," Sasha pointed to two others. "Check it out. Kill him."

Boyd's stomach somersaulted. It could be Vidar. It could be Gabe. It could be any of his teammates, brothers, the men he loved as family. Before he could think more about it, he was tugged toward the first hallway. The sim with Vidar prepared him well for what was coming, but with the power cut, Boyd didn't have to worry too much about infrared. Sasha didn't seem to worry about any of the extra security measures. Boyd had to admit, when the vault came into view, it was anticlimactic. They had been working on the mission for weeks and to just walk through the security, pissed him off. Not to mention he was with Sasha and not Vidar, the man he trained with.

Sasha tugged him forward and tossed him at the vault door. The sounds of gunshots and shouts startled him, but he started working on the combination to open the main door. Sasha shouted something in Russian at his team and two of them came running.

"Vlad and Locke are down but we got one of theirs," they reported.

"Good," Sasha nodded.

"Who?" Boyd demanded, turning from the vault.

"Open the vault," Sasha ordered.

"Not until you tell me who."

Sasha looked at Boyd, annoyance in his eyes, but he glanced at his men and nodded once.

"Some slanty," the man said.

"Slan…" Boyd caught himself. The slur took him a second, but when he understood, he covered his mouth and let out a cry. "Dae…" he breathed.

Chapter Twenty

Vidar raced to Dae's prone form. Even with night vision, he could see his best friend's eyes were closed.

"Dae," he whispered, heart in his throat. "Dae."

Dae's hand twitched and he groaned then his face screwed up before he opened his eyes. *"Ssi-bal."*

Not knowing what he just said in Korean, Vidar let out a breath. At least he was talking. Relief raced through him. Dae looked up at him. "Fuck, I got shot."

"The vest caught it," Vidar whispered and helped him up. Dae groaned as he stood.

"Gare won't let me live this down," he chuckled and took a breath wincing slightly.

"All right?" Vidar questioned. Dae nodded and rolled his neck.

"What happened?"

"I got two of them."

"Thor, Eclipse, come in," Kiter's voice came over their earpieces.

"Go for duo," Vidar said.

"You boys all right?" He asked.

"Affirmative, vest caught it," Vidar explained.

"Good, they've reached the vault. Boyd is refusing to do anything else until he speaks to you. They've already punched him a few times. Not sure what more they'll do, but don't put it past him."

Vidar's fist clenched and his entire arm shook. "Put him through."

"Transferring."

He heard the click and spoke. "Boyd?"

"Baby?" He heard Boyd's voice. "I'm so sorry about Dae."

"Shh shh, it's okay. He's a bit like Lazarus." Vidar hoped Boyd's Catholic orphanage upbringing let him understand the message.

"Baby?" Boyd said softly.

"I'm here."

"...Now there's only three of them."

Vidar heard Sasha curse in Russian, then the unmistakable sound of a fist colliding with a face and the phone went dead.

"Scorpio?" He called for Kiter.

"Your man just punched Sasha," Kiter stated with some humor.

"A One-Two just like we practiced," Callum offered. "It was

fucking awesome."

Kiter, Callum, Nigel, and Marjorie were watching Live CCTV while Gabe, Rhys, and Gareth covered the exits.

"You good?" Vidar checked with Dae, who nodded. "Let's roll."

With their military grade weapons in hand, they made their way cautiously through the hallways toward the vault.

"What the hell is in this vault? And why does he want it so badly?" Dae whispered.

"Evidence of his involvement? Hell, it might be the missing key we're looking for to know who the mastermind is. We're going to have to see," Vidar answered.

"Bogey coming at your twelve o'clock," Callum said over their earpiece.

Vidar and Dae pulled up and sank into the darkness of the wall. They watched as the man ran past them. Vidar nodded at Dae who stepped out and turned toward the man. One shot was all it took, and the man went down, the bullet severing his spine.

The closer they got to the open vault door, the louder the sounds became, and Vidar's anger grew tenfold. Boyd was holding his own. He was no match for Sasha. But he still fought. Every punch reverberated through Vidar's body. There was a pause and Vidar heard Boyd spitting, then laughing.

"What's wrong, Sash? Can't keep at it? I remember your stamina lacked a bit in Transylvania too. Now my man? He's able to satisfy me all night long." Boyd let out a grunt as the thud of a fist hitting a torso drifted down the hall. "Come on, that all you got?"

"Shut up," Sasha retorted. Then, "go see what's taking Wells so long. And get your asses back here." The sound of running footsteps drew their attention and they sank back into the darkness.

"Reaper, coming your way," Vidar said letting the man run down the corridor.

"Finally," Gabe answered over the comms. "Some action."

Dae tapped Vidar on the shoulder and moved his hand in signals they used on their SRR team. He was offering to go low and take out Sasha's knees while Vidar got a shot to knock him down. Dae would watch him while Vidar got Boyd out of there and the team would come in to take Sasha away. Vidar agreed to the plan and with a breath, they lurched forward only for Vidar to hear, "hold, Thor," from Kiter.

Boyd began to speak. "So," he drawled. "I know the number, Do you?" Boyd asked. Sasha grunted. "Eloquently said. That's the only reason you haven't pulled the trigger on the gun you have. If you want my help, get that thing out of my face."

"You think your friends will save you so you're playing tough. But I have news for you, малыш, the second they breach that door, your head explodes with a .45 through your skull. You heard that?" He called out louder.

"You honestly think I'm afraid of you?" Boyd asked. "You think you can rough me up a bit and wave that thing in my face and I'll fall to my knees and beg for mercy? Do you have any concept of what I went through as a kid? I've looked monsters in the face and endured. You're no monster. All I see is a bully. I see a killer. But I also see a puppet. You are just as much in the dark as I am. Admit it." There was a pause. "We might be able to help you, Sash," Boyd's voice was genuine, and Vidar gripped his gun tighter.

"You think a few pretty words will distract me?" Sasha

asked. "I know they're closing in on me. You're my insurance, but I don't have to listen to this."

"Just tell me who you're working for. I promise, my team will look better on this, and you might even be sparred."

"Forget it."

There was another pause. "You don't know, do you? You don't know who you work for. You want the contents of that vault as much as we do for basically the same reasons."

Another pause and Vidar wished he could see Boyd. Let him know he was there. He wanted to see him. Needed to make sure he was all right. But Boyd was getting good information and Vidar had to wait, even if every fiber of his being wanted to run inside, grab Boyd, and take him away.

"Kyetti recruited me," Sasha said. "But he never told me who he worked for. All I know is that it's some MI6 higher up. Kyetti left me when he was released from your custody. Killed his solicitor and fled. I figure if I know who he worked for, I could offer better deal."

"And if he told you to call the Rentai Cartel on my team, killing agents, would you?" Another pause. "Don't forget your allegiance is to the UK."

"My allegiance is to whoever is paying me. I've killed more agents than years you've been alive, малыш."

"Including Darius and Hesler?"

"No... they are not on kill list. They were terminated by someone else."

"Who?" Boyd demanded.

"That's what I want to know, but my opinion is Kyetti called them. He has contacts in the Yakuza."

"But you did kill Hannah."

"Hannah?" Sasha sounded genuinely confused.

"The MI6 undercover agent with the FSB."

"I don't know any Hannah."

"You shot her in the back while she downloaded a list of names and was sending the information. Names of agents who had been killed," Boyd pressed. "She figured out it was you, didn't she?"

"I don't know any Hannah," he said again.

Silence met them and Vidar strained to hear.

"She was married," Boyd's soft voice said.

"So were many I killed," Sasha stated.

"Why, Sash?" Boyd questioned. "Why do you want to live like this?"

"It's all I've ever known."

"There's more to life than this. Don't you want to fall in love? Have a family? Go legit?"

"No, no, and I already am, in that order," Sasha said. "Every kill was sanctioned by the British government."

"That can't be. The government would never kill their own assets."

"*Every* kill was sanctioned by the British government. They're only assets if they stay that way. I've killed for less in the name of the government. It's the cost of National Security. Now, shut up and find the right locker. And where the hell is Tiberius?"

"Sorry to be the barer of bad news," Boyd snipped. "But you're on our turf now, Sasha. And you should never have let me talk to Vidar."

There was a scratching screech of metal grating on metal and then a grunting cry of pain.

"Go, go, go," Kiter ordered.

Vidar didn't hesitate. He and Dae stormed the vault. Dae took out Sasha's knee and as soon as Boyd was a safe distance away, Vidar shot Sasha's arm knocking the gun out of his hand. It skidded across the floor and came to a stop at the base of the lockboxes.

Vidar knew Dae would monitor Sasha and he raced to Boyd who was on the floor, his back resting against the wall. Vidar knelt before him. "Baby?"

Boyd turned tired eyes on him and smiled softly. "I hoped you were out there."

Vidar passed a shaking hand over his head. "I will always be there."

"I know."

"How hurt are you? Can you stand?"

Boyd nodded and tried to get up but leaned heavily against Vidar, his eyes closing. Vidar took quick stock of his injuries but paused when he saw the blood on his black shirt, near his hip. Pressing his hand against it, Boyd reared up and hissed.

"He had a knife," Boyd said simply.

Vidar's eyes flashed to Dae in time to see Sasha move. "Dae!" He shouted, but it was too late. Sasha slashed Dae's leg. His best friend cried out and went down. Blood poured dangerously fast from the wound.

Sasha grabbed Dae's side arm and in one smooth motion, aimed at Boyd. Time stood still as Vidar watched and reached for his gun. He didn't think he was fast enough, but he grabbed his favorite 9mm Sig from his back holster.

Pulling back from Boyd, he kept one arm around him preventing him from falling. He didn't need to worry. Boyd turned toward Sasha too and resting against Vidar's chest, he extended his right arm. Vidar saw the shining .45 in his lover's hand. Boyd had picked up Sasha's own gun where it had fallen when he and Dae attacked.

Without hesitation, he fired. Boyd fired. Together, they eliminated the threat and Vidar took a small amount of pleasure from seeing Sasha's stunned face as he fell backwards in a pool of his and Dae's blood.

There was a split second of silence, then Boyd fell into him. Vidar held him and shouted into his earpiece. "Man down, man down, man down." Dae was holding his leg; the blood didn't seem to stop.

"Go," Boyd said. Vidar helped Boyd sit. He was hurt, bleeding some but Dae's femoral artery had been cut. He'd bleed out in seconds. Rushing to his best friend, he grabbed his belt and tied it above Dae's wound.

Crying out, Dae banged his head against the interior vault door and moaned. *"Gaejasik,"* he muttered.

"Hey now, no language like that." Vidar tried to lighten the mood. "You'll be fine."

"Remind me, next time you ask for my help to punch you in the face," Dae said.

"At least your humor hasn't bled out."

"Sod off," he moaned but Vidar heard the playfulness, and he breathed a silent sigh of relief. He would never have forgiven himself if something worse had happened.

Gareth, Rhys, and Gabe raced in. Sliding on his knees to his husband, he passed a hand over his face.

"I'm okay," Dae breathed and rested his forehead against Gare's.

"Saranghaeyong," Gareth said *I love you* in Korean.

"Nado saranghae," Dae replied and kissed him before pulling back and groaning as EMTs rushed in.

Vidar looked up at Kiter who had arrived with the medical personnel. He walked over. "All right?"

Vidar nodded and turned to look at Boyd who was standing, staring at a specific door. "Baby?"

Boyd turned slowly; his wince told Vidar the adrenaline was wearing off. Walking over, Vidar reached for him. A flash of a smile crossed Boyd's lips but he took Vidar's hand and turned back to the vault door.

"The blood stopped. I think he only just caught me. I'm okay. Sore but I've handled worse. Boss, Vi, it's this the one," he said softly. "The vault we've been looking for, training for. It's much bigger than I expected."

"It's a door," Vidar and Kiter looked at what Boyd indicated. FCEE290717 stared back at them.

"We can't," Kiter said. Boyd turned furrowed brows toward him.

"What do you mean?"

Kiter sighed. "In order to ensure your safety, I had to go to Lester who went to the Deputy Secretary. In exchange for pulling their guards and letting us have control over the system, they ordered me to leave everything alone in the vault. I had to make the deal."

"We're right here. It's what we've trained for. Darius and Hesler lost their lives for this team. We owe it to them, boss!" Boyd was getting more and more animated. "All the evidence is right here. You can't... you... you can't."

"It's out of my hands, Boyd. I was given the stand down order. *I* cannot disturb anything in this vault. *I* have to abide by what *I* promised." Kiter stared at Boyd. It didn't take him long to figure out what their boss meant, and the corner of Boyd's lip tipped up, and it lifted Vidar's heart. "Now, *I* am going to check on the team and make sure Dae is all right. *I* am leaving the vault alone. *I* have touched nothing."

Boyd nodded. "Yes, *you* haven't. We'll be right behind you, boss."

Kiter nodded crisply once and walked out of the main vault following the EMTs, Gareth, and Dae on the gurney. Boyd turned to Vidar and a soft smile lifted his lips.

"It's surreal," he said.

Vidar agreed. "It's what we trained for. It's what *you* trained for. So, go on, baby," he winked. "I'll cover you."

Boyd let out a laugh and turned toward the vault. Reaching forward, he spun the dial and quickly figured out the code. Placing the makeshift lock pick he had into the key slot, he turned the handle and Vidar let out the breath he was holding when the latch resounded in the room. Boyd was breathing slowly, steadily, deliberately.

After a beat, he opened the door.

Chapter Twenty-One

The room that greeted them was dark, but Vidar found the switch on the wall. As soon as the light came on, Boyd gasped and saw Vidar follow his gaze. Eyes wide, he stared at a slumped figure in the chair. Restrained by ropes and a chain, the man was badly beaten. Boyd watched; he was breathing. Rushing over, they checked the man. Vidar lifted his head and Boyd froze.

"Vi," he let out.

Vidar nodded once. "Kyetti."

The man moaned and moved slightly. Boyd hurried around him to the man's back and tugged at the ropes that bound him.

"Wait," Vidar cautioned. "We don't know what is going on."

"We can't leave him like this. I know what this man has done, but this is ridiculous. And he could tell us what we need to know. It's no wonder Sasha wanted in this room. Do you think he knew?"

"Maybe, maybe not," Vidar said. "But pause just for a moment. Check the filing cabinet, see what else is here. They've been guarding this vault long before Kyetti disappeared. Trust me? He's secondary right now."

Boyd nodded and Vidar placed a quick kiss on his lips. He couldn't help himself.

"Let's look around quickly."

They did. Boyd opened the filing cabinet and grabbed out a couple of files. But everything was in code. He reached for his phone and cursed.

"What's wrong?" Vidar asked.

"My phone. I need pictures."

"Sasha have it?"

"I think so."

Vidar left the vault and returned a few seconds later with his phone. Boyd kissed him and opened the camera app. Flipping pages, he snapped pictures. Stuffing the files back in the cabinet, he reached for the next ones when he paused.

Darius, Winstone

Hesler, Richard

He swallowed and took a breath. His friends. The agents they lost nearly half a year ago. The first agents in The Charing Cross Boys apart from Callum and him. The ones killed by the Rentai Cartel in the Maldives.

Slowly removing the files, Boyd opened them. Seeing their handsome faces made a sob crawl out of his throat. Vidar was at his side in an instant but said nothing. A solid, warm, loving hand settled on his lower back and Boyd shook himself.

"We don't have time," he said. Taking pictures as fast as he could, he didn't give himself a second look at their faces. They continued taking as many pictures of the files as possible until someone groaned. Boyd's head whipped around toward Kyetti who was starting to stir. Boyd and Vidar waited and watched as the prisoner opened his eyes. The unfocused orbs fell on them.

"Water, please," his voice was gravelly, and Vidar pulled out a water bottle from his tactical gear. Unscrewing the lid, he held the opening to Kyetti's lips. The man gulped but Vidar pulled it away. "No, please."

"You can have more later. But too much isn't good in your state. You're going to answer some questions and then you can have some water."

Kyetti huffed. "A bit more water first then, please."

Vidar agreed and allowed him to drink once more. "Clock's ticking. We don't have long. Speak. What's going on here? Who is behind the attacks on our team?" Boyd questioned. "Who called the Rentai Cartel? Who do you and Sasha work for?"

"I don't know who he is," Kyetti said. Vidar sighed and poured out some water onto the vault floor. "I-I only have a code name. Roman. But he's part of the government. MI6 probably."

Vidar gave him a sip of water. "Why *probably?*"

"Because he has connections. He told me he called the Rentai Cartel on your team. You were an inconvenience. He didn't want anyone so close to the truth."

"What truth?"

"I don't know," he answered sarcastically. "We didn't exactly go out for tea and scones."

Vidar poured out some more water. "Wait! Okay. He's getting money from both sides. Rentai pays him when any of their most wanted is found. Hassan Petra promised them exclusivity with the nuclear information but when the MI6 agent shot Petra off the Thames, the cartel thought he was dead. When they found out he wasn't and had reneged on the deal, Petra found himself at the top of Rentai's most wanted list." Vidar let him drink again.

"Is this person after our boss or the agent who shot Petra?" Vidar asked.

"Both from my understanding. I was told to reactivate Sasha again before I was captured to try to get close to him. Get information from the team to use against him so he'd come willingly."

"Do you know which agent on our team?" Boyd asked. CCB knew, Callum had revealed it was him over two weeks ago, but he was curious if Kyetti knew.

"Only that he went by the name Ash."

Ash Tree, Fraxinus. Callum. *So he doesn't know.*

"Did you know we were coming for you?" Boyd asked.

"I was told there was a team out for me and to let them capture me. That I would be held in MI6 headquarters while Sasha gathered information on the team after you went to Transylvania. The contents in the safe there are my own personal business. I'd appreciate it if you would stop trying to crack the code."

"We already did. At least, layer one. What does the Latin mean?" Boyd asked.

"What Latin?"

"All things end in truth and in truth you will find the end,"

"Exactly what it means. The truth will come to light but when it does, the house of cards will tumble."

"How did you communicate with this Roman?" Vidar asked.

"Smoke signals," Kyetti snarked. Vidar poured out more water. "Wait! I had a burner phone. We both have one. He rarely called, paranoid I'd hear his voice. But he sent coordinates for locations and all names and dates were coded." Kyetti drank more from Vidar's water bottle.

"A Pig Pen Cipher?" Boyd asked.

"One of the ways, yes. He knew I coded all of my information that way, so it was easy. Whoever he is, he doesn't trust technology apart from sending texts."

"If the information you sent us to get in Transylvania was your own information, why did you send us there?" Vidar asked.

"Because not all of it is. And I was told to. He told me to give you the wrong code so you'd be captured and the microchip in the safety deposit box would be destroyed."

"What's on it?"

"All of my notes on him. All of the messages we sent each other all of the information he gave me. I made a backup. Money transfers, instructions, double coded."

"What's the second level code?" Vidar demanded.

Kyetti looked pointedly down to the water bottle and Vidar rolled his eyes giving him a drink.

"It's a Vigenère Cipher. Let me out of here and I'll give you the code word. I swear to you, I want this person more than anyone. He double bluffed me. I was supposed to be let go when I finished my part. The solicitor was working for Roman too. But they caused the accident and murdered him right before my eyes. Then I was dragged down here, beaten and left to rot. I'll help you. Just get me out of here!"

"That's not up to us," Vidar closed the water bottle and put it in his pouch.

"You need me!"

"Actually, we don't," Vidar said.

"Please!" Kyetti shouted as they stepped out of the inner vault door. "Don't leave me down here."

"We'll take it up with our boss and see. But you've outlived your usefulness, Kyetti," Vidar said.

"Don't leave me in here!" His voice faded as Vidar shut the door.

Ignoring the pleas of a man doomed to die, was not easy. Boyd stared down at Sasha's body, trying to wrestle with his conscience.

"Are you all right?" Vidar whispered, walking over to him. His arms came around him and Boyd leaned back into his chest.

"I thought it'd feel different. I thought revenge would help, but now, all I can think of is how two families and this team will be forever changed by the actions of someone so close to us. The deaths of two agents tossed us from a new team, just stretching our wings, to a vengeful entity who constantly has to look over our shoulder, suspicious of everyone. *Everyone,* Vi. I don't know who I can trust. I don't know how to help save this team."

Vidar gently turned Boyd around to face him. "You can trust me. You can trust our brothers, Kiter, Rhys, Callum, Gabe, Nigel. You can trust us, baby. You are not alone."

Boyd swallowed hard and rested his forehead on Vidar's collarbone. He was so tired. "I'm taking you to the hospital to get checked out. Then, you're going to sleep, and we'll attack the day tomorrow."

Boyd nodded and slipped his arms around Vidar's middle

smiling when his man's arms encircled him. He breathed in Vidar's scent. Cologne overpowered by sweat and man. His man.

"Hospital, then take me home, Jørgensen. I need you. I want you so badly."

Vidar kissed his forehead and did just that.

Chapter

Twenty-Two

Boyd slowly woke in Vidar's bed. His flat was closer to the hospital than Boyd's and with the pain meds they gave him for the bruised ribs and cut on his hip where Sasha's knife had caught him, he was falling asleep in the car when Vidar had swung by Dae and Gare's house to pick up Sheila since they were both at the hospital. He remembered bits and pieces of Vidar picking him up out of the car and holding him to his chest as he carried him to the lift. The feeling of a soft pillow against his throbbing cheekbone was next and eventually the warmth and comfort from Vidar's body as he slipped in beside him.

Boyd took a breath as deeply as he could without pain. He had gotten some good hits in and was pleased when he saw

Sasha's bloody mouth. But the Russian had bulk Boyd could only dream of and struck him repeatedly in the torso. A wave of guilt passed over him as he remembered pulling the trigger, killing Sasha. Sasha had used him. He felt dirty still. Like he was back at the orphanage, but it was his first kill. He kept seeing the scared look in Sasha's eyes like he was trying to figure out who double crossed him. Those eyes morphed to Jack's, and then to all the boys in the orphanage. Then Sasha became the warden in his mind's eye and Boyd couldn't breathe.

No, no no, no, he chanted to himself. *I'm not there. I'm safe. Sasha isn't McMasters. I'm not a kid anymore. I'm safe.*

"Boyd?" That voice, he knew it and latched onto it. "Boyd? Baby? Are you okay?

Breathe, breathe, breathe.

"Boyd?"

"P... pa... panic..."

"Panic attack?"

Boyd nodded. Vidar was there. He had to remember. His lover's lips pressed against his temple, his forehead, his nose, cheekbones. Vidar moved. Lips pressed softly to Boyd's, and he sighed into his boyfriend's mouth. The panic attack slowly receded, and he was able to take a deep breath.

"Better," he breathed. Sheepishly, he looked up at Vidar. "Sorry. What a way to wake up, huh?"

"Was it because of last night? Sasha?" Vidar asked.

Boyd nodded. "I feel so dirty knowing what I let him do to me. What I *wanted* him to do to me. And then guiltier still knowing I killed him."

"It's in the past, baby. He's dead. He can never hurt you like that again. You're safe. You were able to take care of yourself. I'm so proud of you. Dae and I heard, and Callum's voice was filled with pride as he told me what he was seeing, how you were fighting."

"Dae... how is he? Is he okay? They said they killed him."

"Vest caught it," Vidar explained. "But I checked on him in the hospital while they were taking you for the MRI. He's expected to make a full recovery. He lost a lot of blood, but they were able to take care of everything. Gareth and his parents are with him."

"I'm so glad. I was so worried," he said.

"I know baby. He immediately asked how you were when I entered his room."

Boyd buried his smile into Vidar's shoulder. "It's nice to have friends. It's been a while."

Vidar kissed his temple. "You'll always have friends now, Baby."

"Mm," he burrowed into Vidar's side. "That's nice."

Vidar kissed his temple. "Sleep. I need to take Sheila outside. I'll be right back. Rest."

"Mmhmm," he sighed and fell back to sleep before feeling Vidar leave.

The next time he woke up, it was to the smell of coffee and a breakfast fry. Two of his favorite things. He was alone in bed, but he slowly sat up, his head still a bit groggy and his ribs were tender. But his bladder was screaming at him. Getting up and staying on his feet was more difficult than he expected. Falling back onto his bed once too many times, Boyd finally made his way to the toilet. Once he was finished, he tugged on one of Vidar's soft undershirts. It smelled too much of laundry detergent, so Boyd found the cologne and sprayed a squirt onto the white cotton. Taking a deep breath of the clean crisp scent, he smiled, wincing a little at the tug of his busted lip, and headed out to the main room. Sheila barked and bounded over to him.

"Hey sweet baby," Boyd cooed and slowly crouched to pet her. She licked his face and pushed her head onto his shoulder as if giving him a hug.

"She was worried about you. She stayed right by the door until I started frying up some bacon. Then, that had all of her attention," Vidar's voice came from the kitchen and soon he appeared, a soft smile on his face.

"Of course," Boyd teased still petting her soft fur. "I borrowed one of your shirts. Hope you don't mind."

"Not at all, I like you in my clothes," Vidar replied and walked over to him, helping him to his feet.

"What time is it?"

"Just gone 1230. You needed to sleep. I was on the phone with the team. They're all glad you're all right and Kiter said for us to report in whenever you're back on your feet. We can take the day if you want."

With Vidar's help, Boyd sat on the sofa. "I don't think we should. I think we need to talk to the team about Kyetti."

"They went over the tapes. Our comms were still on, they heard everything. Gabe and Callum went to get him from the vault. He's currently in our custody at HQ."

"Oh good." Boyd looked up at his lover again and stared. But his emotions were winning, and his throat was thickening.

Vidar crouched in front of him. "What's wrong?"

"How do you do it?"

"Do what?" Vidar asked.

"How do you live with yourself after taking a life? I know Sasha was bad. I get it. But I killed him."

Vidar took a breath. "I've always had to look at it as war. My country sent me to protect innocent people. People who didn't want war and death, only a few of their leaders did. There are so many good people in this world but there are a few bad ones and usually it's the bad ones who run the state. I saw so many men, women, and children who died, a victim of their circumstances. They didn't want war. They didn't want to try and kill me. And the ones who did, sometimes didn't know better. Did that make them bad? No. Did it make them evil? No. But they were pawns used by bad and evil men who made money off war.

"Sasha was troubled. He thought he was doing what he was charged with by his country. But hurting you, hurting Dae, killing Marjorie's wife, killing our agents abroad, that was a choice he made and a choice that ultimately got him killed. I take out the personal and replace it with the facts. The first time I killed someone," Vidar looked away. "You never will forget. It will be branded in your mind until the day you either lose your mind or you die. But I'm here. You can always talk to me. I will not judge anything. And if it makes you feel better, you can think your aim was a little off and it was my bullet that killed him. Let me shoulder the burden for you."

Boyd took a breath. "No, it's our burden." He cupped Vidar's jaw and leaned forward to kiss him. Softly, gently, and filled with such love. When he pulled back, he smiled at the handsome face staring at him. "I would kill for you. I would die for you. But I will live for you."

Vidar closed his eyes and took a deep breath. "I love you. And I would do anything for you. Baby..." he paused, seemed to debate, then spoke. "I need to tell you something."

"Okay."

"I'm here. You're safe."

"I know." Boyd's brow furrowed in confusion. "What's going on?"

Again, Vidar let out a breath. "The warden who hurt you, what was his name?"

Boyd swallowed the bile that rose in his chest. "McMasters." Vidar nodded and looked away. "Why?"

On a heaved sigh, Vidar locked eyes with him. "The bill for Prison Reform passed. The first of the prisoners were released this morning. Jacob McMasters was one of them. He's been released."

Boyd's stomach dropped. His ears rang. His chest constricted. He couldn't breathe. His mouth was so dry. His heart beat so fast. His eyes stayed glued on Vidar, but his vision swam and grayed. In an instant, he was back at St. John's with that disgusting man's hands on him. He remembered the pain, the humiliation, the dehumanization, the stolen innocence. He remembered every word spoken, every smell, every whimper, every malicious laugh. His hand itched to reach out to Jack. Jack was his only friend. He'd protect him. *But Jack isn't here.*

"Boyd."

Vidar. Vidar was there. He'd protect him. A wet tongue and a soft whimper and Boyd buried his head into Sheila's fur and let out a scream.

The next thing he remembered, he was on the floor, Sheila was beside him and he was in Vidar's lap.

"Vi?"

"Baby?" Vidar's voice sounded thick. "I'm here. You're

safe."

Boyd nodded slowly. "He won't get to me, will he?"

"Never. I promise you. I will take care of it." And with that promise, he believed him.

Boyd and Vidar arrived at HQ around 0900 the next morning and were greeted by the CCB Team in their offices. With the threat of Sasha eliminated, their families were free to leave the bunker and the boys were back upstairs. Each member of the team embraced Boyd and made sure he was all right. Callum smiled though it didn't reach his eyes and embraced him. He whispered in his ear before he pulled back.

"I saw the press conference about the man who hurt you. Are you all right?" He asked. Boyd nodded thanking his kindred spirit. They had talked more than anyone about what happened to them, and Callum was the only one he believed when he said *I know what you're going through.*

"Vidar's looking into it. But he can't hurt me."

"No, he can't," Callum agreed and pulled back. "I'm here if you need to talk."

"Thank you," Boyd squeezed his arm.

"Glad you're okay, kid," Kiter said coming up next to him.

"Same," he smiled.

"Let's get some coffee and gather in the conference room," Kiter announced.

Once everyone was settled, Kiter began. "Two days ago we were given vital information about the person who betrayed us, causing our team to lose two valuable members. Kyetti is in our custody with 24/7 guard. He gave us important information, naming the codename of the man working against us as *Roman*. Kyetti is our only major link to Roman, whoever it is. So, with that in mind, do we know how to use the information he gave us? Boyd, any luck in cracking the second code on his files?"

"Not yet, boss," he said. "It's a Vigenère cipher so if we don't know the word it won't do much good. I've got it currently running through every word in English, but do we think it will be in English? Or will it be in Kyetti's language? Or even Latin?"

"Have you tried Roman?" Callum asked.

Boyd pulled out his laptop and logged in. "No, but I will."

"Do, and let us know," Kiter said. "Now the files you took pictures of held some interesting items. Darius and Hesler's were mainly personnel files. I always assumed the person monitoring us had access to our background information. It appears that's what happened. Boyd, while you were out yesterday, Callum heard your tablet dinging and found this," Kiter pulled up an image of his tablet on the projector.

"My algorithm finished. It should tell us who accessed the personnel files," Boyd explained. "Hit F3 on the keyboard."

Kiter did and the information popped up on the screen.

"Who's Abe Dalal?" Gabe asked.

"The Deputy Secretary's personal assistant. The one who watched the training session and, my guess, added the extra security of Dae's team," Kiter explained. "I had my suspicions of him for a while. The Secretary isn't one to get his hands dirty, if indeed he even knows about it."

"So he pulled the personnel files? Did the secretary order the hit?" Nigel asked. "Why would the secretary want us dead?"

"Let's find out," Kiter began.

"Boss," Boyd called. "Roman didn't work, but I tried it in

Latin; Romanus."

"And?"

Boyd clicked a few times and took over the projection. "Files are open."

The hundreds of folders, files, documents, pictures, and audio files floated on the screen. A hush descended on the team, but it was short lived.

"There," Callum stated. "Folder marked with the date of our mission to arrest Petra."

Boyd clicked on it and more documents including their personnel files showed on the screen. Seeing their faces and two red Xs over Darius and Hesler, Boyd shook with anger.

"Who is this guy?" He demanded.

"That video file, pull it up. On screen," Kiter said. Boyd did and immediately recognized that beach and the man with two M4s firing. Hesler. Darius' body was behind him, and he was struggling to stay on his feet.

"Body cam footage from that day," Callum explained to the rest of the team. "Boyd cams of the Rentai Cartel."

The cartel's men were shouting in a language Boyd didn't know but his eyes were on Hesler as he kept fighting, kept shooting, kept screaming his personal war cry. When he fell backwards over Darius' body, Boyd felt Vidar's hand slip into his. Boyd was sobbing. Trying to get himself under control, Boyd breathed and focused on the video. Detaching the emotional.

"Rhys, what are they saying?" Kiter asked.

"Giving orders," Rhys answered. He had spent most of his childhood in Japan when his father was stationed at Okinawa and spoke Japanese fluently as well as being a black belt in Jujitsu.

Rhys listened and translated. "'We have killed Petra.

Orders complete. Brits dead. Back to the ship. Retreat.' 'What about the ones that got away?' 'No consequence. The Roman will deal with them.'"

"*The* Roman?"

Rhys nodded. "Not a proper name."

"Go on."

"'Make sure they're dead.' 'They are.' 'Let's go.' 'Move it.' 'Wait, she's coming to shore.'"

"She?" Gabe questioned.

"'Why?'" Rhys went on translating. "'Wants to see for herself.' 'No time. They may call reinforcements.' 'No, not likely. They weren't supposed to be here anyway.'"

A female voice spoke next, and Rhys translated. "'Unsanctioned or not, they think they are supposed to be here. The Roman tasked us with sending a message.'" There was a pause, then she continued in English. "Mission complete, message sent. Activate Kyetti."

The body cam turned, and they saw a very beautiful woman, perhaps mid-fifties on the phone.

"Who is that?" Nigel questioned.

Marjorie stood, Boyd noticed her shaking and walked closer to the screen. "Has the tape been tampered with?" She asked.

"What? No, I don't know," Boyd answered.

"Find out!" she shrieked.

Boyd flinched, extracted his hand from Vidar's and began to type.

"Marjorie?" Kiter asked.

"Boyd?" Her voice like a gunshot.

"No, the video is intact," Boyd pronounced, seeing no

evidence of tampering.

"Marjorie," Kiter injected steel into his voice. "Who is it?"

She took a shaking breath, and the silent room heard her swallow hard.

"Hannah."

"Your wife?" Vidar asked.

She nodded but didn't take her eyes off the image of the woman on the beach in Malaysia on the phone.

"She's dead," Boyd said. "You said she's dead."

"She is dead. Her grave is beside my father's. I heard the gunshot. I heard Sasha's voice. I heard her last breath. She is dead!" She was shaking and her voice rose. Kiter rushed to her as she fainted. He caught her. Rhys helped him get her seated and Callum hurried down the steps grabbing the first aid kit off the wall. Finding the smelling salts, he cracked it open and waved it under her nose. She jerked awake. Her eyes found the image of her supposedly dead wife and she whimpered as tears fell down her cheeks.

Kiter took a breath, stepped back up onto the platform in the lecture hall style room. He stared at the woman on the screen and heaved a sigh. Nodded, as if resigned and turned back to the team. The room was quiet apart from Marjorie's sobs.

"Team," Kiter began. "We have lost loved ones, friends, teammates, lovers, in the name of national security. We have been a target from day one. I, for one, want to know why. Everyone has the opportunity to say no. No one is under any obligation. I will not run the team like that. So, that said, if you disagree with me and my plan, do not feel like you have no options. You can come to me, tell me, and you can do as you see fit. I will ask no one to lie for me. You want to go to my superior and report me, do so. And you will suffer no reprisals. But if not, if this team is what I hope it is. I could use every single one of you and some others we might need to bring in. But my hope is that we will discover who Roman is. How Hannah is alive. And why the hell is going on. I will ask each of you your answer. Callum?"

"With you."

"Rhys?"

"Always."

"Boyd?"

"Let's get this son of a bitch."

"Nigel?"

"Not sure what use I'll be, I'm with you."

"Gabe?"

"Yes, I didn't know them, but you have inspired my loyalty. So I'm with you."

"Vidar?"

"The team is my found family. It's not a mission, boss, it's survival. Let's do this."

"Marjorie?"

She took a shuddering breath. "I have to know."

"Then with unanimous consent. We do this."

"What is *this*, boss? What's your plan?" Callum asked.

"We need to get in with the Rentai Cartel and figure out what the hell is going on."

To Be Continued in

THE CHARING CROSS BOYS

Book Four:

Hold Me Closer

Read on for the Epilogue.

Epilogue

Two months later

"I really don't know about this, boys," Boyd said as he followed Nigel, Callum, and their latest recruit down the street toward Rocketman pub.

"Would you relax? It's your birthday. We're going to celebrate," Nigel teased.

"But where's Vi?" Boyd asked.

"He said he'll meet us there. Come on, Dae, Gareth, Kiter, and Rhys are already there," Gabe reminded him.

"But…"

"Oh come on, you can be separated from your boyfriend for a couple minutes. You're not joined at the hip, right?" Nigel asked.

"You're one to talk, Nige," Callum teased. "You've spent a grand total of two hours away from your boyfriend since you got together."

"And never on a birthday, right?" Their newest recruit responded.

"Oh piss off, the lot of you," Nigel winked.

Gabe merely laughed and wrapped his arm around Nigel's waist. It was good to see him walking again. But Boyd knew he would get tired soon. Nigel's broken leg was in a walking cast, but Boyd saw Gabe holding his cane just in case he needed it.

"Vidar said he'll be here soon, just had to finish up his phone call with his mother," Gabe said.

"I would have waited for him," Boyd protested.

"This way we get to have a drink with you on your birthday," the newest recruit said and opened the door to the pub for them.

"Such a gentleman," Boyd teased and walked in. The Rocketman had transformed from the daytime pub to the nightclub and Boyd *loved* it. The lights, sounds, music, and dancers filled him with happiness. Once, he had thought about possibly joining the pole dancers, but decided against it. He preferred to dance only for Vidar.

"There they are," Gabe called over the thumping base.

Sure enough, his team, along with Dae and Gareth sat or stood around one of the bar tops with a half-naked man dancing over them. They cheered when they saw him and a round of *Happy Birthday* echoed in the room. The whole team had already wished him well for his day with cake and lunch, but it seemed they wanted to embarrass him. He blushed but grinned as Rhys moved to stand, giving him his prime seat at the bar. A stunning drag queen walked over with a round of shots and beer.

"Happy birthday, cutie," she said.

"Cheers," Boyd smiled. He always loved seeing how other queens did their makeup and he especially loved her sparkly eyelids. "You look beautiful."

"Oh," she pressed a hand to her amplified cleavage. "Aren't you just the sweetest. I could gobble you up," she patted his cheek.

"His boyfriend might not like that," Rhys teased.

"Don't see him around, do you?" She winked. "Anyway, I'm Miss Ophelia D-lite. You need anything, sugar, you let me know."

"Thanks," Boyd grinned. He loved it, but his eyes kept drifting to the door. *Where are you, Vi?*

"All right, boys," Kiter picked up one of the shots and raised it. The others grabbed theirs. Kiter looked toward Boyd. "Happy 22nd Birthday, Boyd. We are so glad to have you on our team. You are a friend, a comrade, our comedic relief," he chuckled, but didn't deny it. "And a brother. We love you, and we wish you a very Happy Birthday and many happy returns of the day! To Boyd!"

"Boyd!" The team cheered and tossed back the shot.

"Thanks, Kite," Boyd replied. "The last six months have been so crazy. I never thought meeting you, Rhys, would change my life so much."

"Me neither," Rhys chuckled. "Still owe me for that, by the way."

"I'd offer to pay up, but my boyfriend and your husband would probably kill me," Boyd grinned and laughed seeing Kiter slip his arm around Rhys.

"Did I hear someone has a birthday?" Arlo walked over, looking far too good in his black leather pants, black sequence shirt and heavy eyeliner.

"Hey, Arlo," they said as he saddled up between Dae and Callum.

"Boys, always good to see you." He beamed at Dae.

"You remember my husband, Gareth." Dae leaned back so

Arlo could see the Welshman seated beside him.

"I do," Arlo smiled. "Good to see you too. Haven't seen you boys here for the nightclub."

"First time," Gareth replied.

"Oh baby, they'll have fun with that. Wait until our last man *La Mount* dances. He's our best and will be on this very stage." Arlo touched the top of the bar where they sat. "But who's birthday is it?"

"Mine," Boyd answered.

"Oh, splendid! That has earned you a private dance."

"Oh no, thanks, Arlo. I'm waiting for Vidar."

"Tosh, if he's content to leave you to fend for yourself on your birthday, then you have every right to fend for yourself. We have a room available. Come on."

"No really, I'm good."

"Go on," Rhys told him.

"Yeah, we won't tell Vi," Dae teased.

"He shows up, you're in the loo," Gare said.

"Yeah, go on," Callum encouraged.

Boyd never did like peer pressure and the men were all in committed relationships. There was no reason they would encourage him without an ulterior motive. He had a distinct impression where Vidar might be. But he played dumb.

"Okay," he shrugged. The team cheered as he slid off the stood. "You'll tell Vidar?"

"We'll cover for you," Rhys promised.

Boyd followed Arlo to a private room and headed inside.

"Enjoy," Arlo winked and closed the door behind him. There were no windows, even the door was more of an industrial style. The lights were up about thirty-five percent and Boyd found a single chair facing an empty stage. Sighing, he hoped he wasn't wrong. It would be difficult to tell Vidar about it. As soon as he sat, the lights went off.

"Dramatic," he muttered in the absolute darkness. Then, his eyes were drawn to the single white light switched on onstage. A man, backlit by the light, stood, legs spread, one hand on his fedora hat, the other flat against his stomach. Black dancer pants encased his thick legs, and the white button up shirt he wore, strained over his arms and muscles.

Unbuttoned to his mid chest, the shirt looked soft and tantalizing. He wore slip-on men's black jazz shoes and Boyd honestly had never seen anything more attractive. He'd know that body anywhere. He had spent every day of the last few weeks worshiping and exploring every inch. But damn, Vidar looked ridiculously hot.

Then the music started. *Feeling good.* The soft violin music followed by Michael Bublé's sensual voice and Vidar's movement, caused Boyd's pants to suddenly be very tight. He moved slowly, one with the music, up and down the stage, his hips jerking from side to side in a fluid, yet deliberate motion. Boyd watched fascinated as his lover danced for him. Vidar's body moved with such grace. It was stunning.

A little more than halfway through the song, when the music swelled Vidar jumped off the stage and gyrated his way like a big cat dancing toward Boyd. In time with the beat, Vidar gripped Boyd's knees and pushed his legs apart, rolling his torso. Grabbing hold of the chair arms, Vidar pushed his body between Boyd's legs and slid up. Standing over him, he moved with the music touching Boyd everywhere. His sensual moves had Boyd panting, his body tight with want and need, his man put on quiet a show.

As the music died down and came to an end, Vidar again slipped between his knees, kneeling before him. His fingers slid up Boyd's legs and to the belt he wore around his waist. He unbuckled it and with a snap, opened his fly.

"Oh shit," Boyd breathed, harder than he'd ever been before. Vidar had never used his mouth on him. He had promised once, he would give his first blow job on Boyd's birthday. "I'm already so close, baby. I won't last…"

Vidar grinned and pulled him out of his pants. Feeling his lover's rough fingers wrap around his hard length still gave him a jolt, but looking down, he saw Vidar's eyes asking permission. Boyd nodded. No words were exchanged after Boyd's declaration.

Vidar looked down and smirked, then with a quick sexy glance up at Boyd, he swallowed Boyd's length and Boyd cried out. Vidar's mouth was wet, hot, and felt so unbelievably good. Though his technique was a little sloppy, what he lacked in finesse, he made up for in enthusiasm.

Hollowing his cheeks, Vidar sucked up and down Boyd's length. Groaning, Boyd stretched back, thrusting deeper. He felt Vidar's throat convulse around him and he was coming with a shout. Like a champ, Vidar swallowed and slurped up every drop.

Panting, Boyd melted into the chair and watched Vidar stroke himself faster and faster, until he let go on a deep moan. Staring at each other, they both felt the grin spread across their faces. Vidar sat up to his knees and Boyd leaned forward, their lips crashed together. Boyd could taste himself on Vidar's tongue and it made the whole sensation heady. Boyd slipped out of the chair and knelt before Vi. Taking him in his arms, Boyd rested his head on Vidar's chest and breathed him in. Sweat, man, and Vidar. The hint of his cologne was just enough to tease Boyd's nose. Not long ago, Vidar had given Boyd a bottle to keep at his flat. He used it every night Vidar wasn't with him, which wasn't very often.

They were quiet for a long while, just content to hold each other until Vidar kissed his head. "Happy Birthday, baby," he whispered.

Boyd pulled back and smiled at him. "The best birthday ever." The look on Vidar's face warmed him. His dark eyeliner and matte makeup looked amazing framing his laughing blue eyes. He was happy. Boyd loved to see it. "Where on earth did you learn to dance like that?"

"Gareth's sister is a choreographer. I asked for her help. She couldn't agree fast enough. Those were the texts I kept hidden from you.

"The texts from Dae and Arianwen?"

Vidar nodded. "I didn't want you to know. I wanted to surprise you."

"It is a surprise. I knew something was up when the boys encouraged me to accept Arlo's offer of a lap dance. Did they know?"

"Yes, they helped me with the logistics."

Boyd chuckled. "Did they see you dance?"

"No," Vidar shook his head. "Only you, baby... well, and my dance coach."

"She doesn't count, but I would like to thank her. That was the hottest thing ever."

Vidar laughed and Boyd pulled back to see the carefree look on his face. He loved it. After a moment, he asked, "how's your mum?"

"She's good. Can't wait to meet you," Vidar said.

"I'm looking forward to it. Have you heard from your dad?"

"After he was kicked out of the PFA, he went home to Norway. Haven't heard from him since. Don't know where he is. I was approached the other day by *The Daily Mail,* they wanted to interview me about the video."

"And?"

"Oh god no," Vidar answered. "I want nothing to do with any of that."

They held each other in silence for a long moment, until Boyd spoke into his chest. "Thank you."

"For what?" Vidar asked.

"For taking care of McMasters." Boyd didn't need to feel him tense to know he did. Pulling back, he locked eyes with Vidar. "I knew it was you when I heard the news reports of his death. Thank you."

"You're not angry with me?"

"I thought I would be. I thought I should be. But no, I'm not. Thank you."

Vidar nodded slowly. "You're welcome."

"I love you."

Vidar smiled softly. "I love you too."

They held each other tightly until a knock came at the door. Boyd made himself presentable while Vidar cleaned up. Calling for the person to come in, the door opened, and Rhys stuck his head in first, eyes closed.

"Decent?" He called.

"Nothing you haven't seen before," Boyd shot back.

"True, but I'd prefer not to be killed by your boyfriend or remind my husband about that," Rhys teased and entered the room. "Cake's here. Arlo refuses to let us have any until you blow out the candles. But from the smell in here, candles aren't the only things getting blown."

"Don't be jealous just because my man has no gag reflex," Vidar said.

"Who says I'm jealous?" Rhys wiggled his eyes suggestively. "Come on, Birthday Boy." With that, Rhys left the room.

Without thinking, they reached for each other's hands and Boyd beamed. Vidar used to say Boyd was a nymph casting a spell on him, but Boyd knew better than that. It was Vidar. Who put a spell on him, and Boyd hoped he never broke it.

Acknowledgements

Thank you all so much for reading!

I have loved Boyd Falstaff since the beginning of *The Charing Cross Boys* book one *Set Fire to the Rain.* He has been such a fun character to write, though his childhood was a very difficult subject. The boys have their origins in *Love Among the Shamrocks Collection, The Next Generation You Don't Own Me,* which will be Callum's and Killian's story. I started writing it first but as soon as I wrote the characters I knew they had some sort of history and thus this series began.

If you are interested in some of the external aspects of this book, please take a look at the series *Love Among the Shamrocks Collection, The Next Generation* and *Love Among the Shamrocks Universe Take My Breath Away* is Peter and Geoff's story and parts of it takes place during this time. You get to meet the SRR team and learn more about their commander Geoff.

Funny story is, in the original draft of *Love Among the Shamrocks Collection The Song of Heart's Desire* Peter was gay and in a relationship with a Viking named Vidar. That relationship didn't work and Vidar was changed to Vivian. Then Peter and Geoff's story took flight. But I loved the name Vidar and his character so much that I wanted to use him. In *Take My Breath Away* I named one of the SRR teams Vidar in homage to him. Never did I think Vidar would be the one Kiter took to the party as a fake date in *Set Fire to the Rain* and in so doing he would join the CCB Team and get his Happily Ever After!

I wanted to thank my cousin, Alex, for his military expertise in helping me make the military parts as accurate as I could. Thank you for your service. I love you, brother! Stay safe! I also wanted to thank my beta readers for their contribution and support.

This book was very difficult to write as the subject matter was tough. Boyd went through so much as a child and to have your mind filled with those horrible situations tears you down. I was in a very dark place already due to personal issues and this nearly drowned me. I have to thank my parents for their love and support during this very difficult time. You mean so much to me and I couldn't imagine going through this tough time without you!

I hope you loved Boyd and Vidar as much as I did! Please consider leaving a review on your favorite site and don't forget to follow me on social media under the handle M. Katherine Clark Author! And be sure to sign up for my newsletter at www.mkatherineclark.net! Keep an eye out for my next release. *The Charing Cross Boys* was only supposed to be four books but of course, as it goes, it will now be five. My next book will follow the storyline with CCB and will feature Dae-Hyun and Gareth... and Elton?? I can't wait to share Book Four of the series; *The Charing Cross Boys: Hold Me Closer.*

About the Author

I absolutely loved working on this book and am so grateful to be able to be living my dream life! I have enjoyed so many wonderful events meeting new readers and catching up with current fans! There is always more content to share so be sure to sign up for my newsletter on my website.

M. Katherine Clark is a Butler University Graduate and an Indiana Native. Writing since she could put pencil to paper at a young age, she credits her mother's influence and support for her head in the clouds and feet firmly on the ground. Ever since she was a child she has been fascinated with reading and the ability to create worlds in your head. When she discovered she could make it a career, well, the rest was history! A daughter, sister, aunt, cousin, and niece, M. Katherine Clark loves spending time with her family and tries not to bore them with too much information about her upcoming books! She lives on social media. If she isn't posting, she's constantly checking for updates (anything to escape writing! Oops, did I write that out loud?)

Be sure to check out her other works and though she can never answer which is her favorite since it would be like picking a favorite child, she hates to be pigeonholed and has a little something for everyone! Signed paperbacks and hardbacks for some titles are available for order on her website and through social media! If you message her and can tell her what the name of the Miley Cyrus song Boyd uses in his dance for Vidar, you get an additional 5% off your order!